MELTED COLD
A COLLECTION OF SHORT STORIES

TONY ORTIZ

EDITED BY THE PRO BOOK EDITOR

COVER DESIGN BY NOEL SELLON

"A NIGHT OUT" STORY IDEA BY DAVID ORTIZ

BOOKS BY THE AUTHOR

Make Way for You – Tips for Getting Out of Your Own Way

Fractal – A Time Travel Tale (A Novel)

Check out the following for even more reading:

Free-Writing: www.SpunToday.com/freewriting

Short Stories: www.SpunToday.com/shortstories

For David

"Have your opinion, don't let your opinion have you."
— *Patrice O'Neal*

A NIGHT OUT

"So what's this place supposed to be, exactly? Like a hibachi spot?" I asked.

"No, nothing like that," replied Jaime. "You cook your own food. They bring whatever you order out to you, fresh and organic. And you sit in private booths that have a little stovetop in the middle."

"So you want to go to a restaurant and pay them to let us cook our own food?" I quipped.

"Stop it. It's part of the charm. You'll see," she replied. "And the drinks are supposed to be amazing."

"Great, so we'll be paying even more to go out and cook our own food. Are we picking up your brother?" I asked.

"No, he and Maria are just going to meet us there after work," Jaime replied.

"Okay, cool. I was thinking of inviting Christian too. He's been dating a new girl, so might be down to triple date," I replied.

"Yea, sure. I like Christian," Jaime replied. "Whatever you want, hun. It's your day."

"I'll call him," I added as I got comfortable on the couch.

While Jaime went into the bedroom to undoubtably spend way too much time picking out an outfit for the evening, I hit up Chris while flipping through TV channels.

"Birthday boy, what's going on?" Christian said when he picked up the call.

"Chris, what's up, bro?" I asked.

"Not much. Looking to wrap things up here at work within a couple of hours," he replied. "You?"

"Nothing much," I said. "Took off today and going to dinner tonight at seven. Some spot Jaime picked out."

"Nice," Christian stated.

"Are you still with that girl you told me about?" I asked. "Let's triple date."

"Yeah, things are going pretty well too," Christian replied. "I'm down for that. Who else is going?"

"Just us, Carlos and Maria," I answered.

"Nice. Okay, cool. Text me the spot, and we'll meet you there," he said.

"Sounds good. Peace." I hung up my cell and set it on the coffee table, then turned my attention back to the TV.

A few guilty pleasures later, including indulging in the *Back to the Future* trilogy, and about seventeen of Jaime's outfit changes later, melted that afternoon away. It was a cold night, so luckily, we didn't have to wait in a line outside before getting into the restaurant.

My girl stepped up to the hostess station and told the maître d', "Hi, we have a seven o'clock reservation. Under Jaime."

"Jaime for six?" he asked.

"Yup, that's us," she replied.

"Would you like to wait by the bar for the rest of your party or go to the table?" he asked.

Turning to me, Jaime asked, "What do you think, babe?"

"The table is fine. They should be here soon, anyway," I replied.

We looked around as the maître d' gathered up menus and linen napkin rolls of silverware. The restaurant was bustling. It had a dark, smokey look that was both sleek and quaint.

"Oh, look, there's Maria by the bar already," Jaime said, then she waved her over, indicating our table was ready.

"Hey, guys," Maria said as she came over with an exotic drink in hand. "Happy birthday, Benny."

"Happy birthday, my guy," added Carlos.

"Thanks, thanks," I responded.

"Here, hold on to this," Carlos said as he handed me an Old Fashioned.

"Jaime, you have to order this drink called the Blue Midnight, or something like that," Maria started.

"It's Blue Velvet," Carlos corrected. "See, she's drunk already," he added jokingly.

"Whatever," Maria responded. "The point is, it's so good that I want to reverse engineer the shit to make it at home."

The maître d' showed us to our table as two of the wait-staff pulled out Jaime and Maria's chairs.

"Who else is coming?" asked Carlos as he saw the six seats.

"Oh, I invited Christian," I replied. "He's supposed to come with this new girl he's been dating."

While our dapperly dressed waiter was still passing out the menus, Jaime put in a family-style appetizer order based on what she'd read was best reviewed. Right then Christian and his girl made their way to our table.

"Hey, everybody, this is Carolina," Christian announced. "That's the birthday boy, and I'm sure you'll catch everyone else's name eventually."

Jaime glared at him. "Boy, don't you have any home training? You know better than that." Then she turned to his date with a welcoming smile and said, "Hi, Carolina, I'm Jaime, this is Maria and her husband Carlos, who is also and unfortunately my brother. I kid, I kid."

Carolina met everyone's gaze as she replied, "Hey, everybody. It's so nice to finally meet you." Then to Jaime she said, "So that must make you the one with the good taste to pick this place."

"You don't have to be nice and lie to her," I chimed in, laughing.

"No, honest, I heard the drinks here are amazing," Carolina said as she and Christian took their seats.

"I'm just playing," I replied. "They are pretty good. I can't front."

Some nights just hit the memory banks differently. You know the type. When every detail of the evening vibes perfectly with the next. From the company to the conversation, the happiness and genuine laughter. This was one of those nights. Before long we were just glassy-eyed staring at the leftover desserts on the table, feeling perfectly satiated by food and drink.

"Is it just me or was everything delicious?" asked Maria.

"I liked it all too," I added. "Great pick, babe. Thank you."

"Aww, I'm glad you did, babes," Jaime responded. "I'd definitely come here again."

"Yea, same," we all seemed to have simultaneously said in agreement.

Christian walked back over from the restroom. "Yo,

we're about to shut this place down. It's a ghost town. Nobody's even on the other side," he said.

"Yea, let's break out," replied Carlos.

Our waiter approached the table. "I trust you enjoyed your experience tonight?" he asked.

"We did. Thank you very much," Jaime replied.

"If you all would oblige," started the waiter, "Mr. Shinto would like to treat you all to one more complementary, off menu drink in his VIP lounge."

With nods of excitement, we all agreed and then followed him toward the back walled area, which had a speakeasy style concealed door leading to the VIP lounge. We really hadn't noticed how deserted the place was until then, like it had been closed for hours.

We walked through and into a dimly lit room filled with artwork, sculptures, and antiques. Passing the empty tables and booths, we headed straight for the bar at the other end of the room where a dozen drinks had been lined up for us. We each enjoyed them while walking around the room, looking at an array of fascinating finds.

"Hey, check this out," Carolina told Christian. "It's a Monet."

"Wow, it seems legit too," he replied.

"Not seems. Is. When I say it's a Monet, I mean it's a Monet," she added.

"Get the fuck out of here," said Carlos, noticeably sauced up. "That ain't real."

"Since when do you know about art?" Maria interjected.

"I'm just saying," replied Carlos. "Who has that? And what would it be doing in the back room of a restaurant?"

"Dude, did you see what's behind that memorabilia case?" I asked Carlos. "There are stacks of PSA 10 rookie cards, including multiples of Kobe, Jordan, Mantle, Gretzky, LeBron. There's a Pete Maravich for God's sake."

"I get it," replied Carlos. "That's nothing to sneeze at. But that's not the same as a Monet."

"Bro, she majored in Art," said Christian. "She knows what she's talking about."

"Minored," Carolina corrected. "Not majored. But it is a passion of mine, and I can tell you with the highest degree of certainty that Claude Monet himself painted that canvas. It's actually one of his earlier works. Pay attention to his use of natural light within the frame. Seemingly unremarkable, until you notice his use of shadows and dark tonal shades. He's masterful in showing how the moonlight embraces each reachable crevice of the landscape. His brush strokes are reminiscent of a time when he only worked in charcoal and the frequency of the bristles on the canvas echo the speed of those strokes, which is signature Monet."

"I bet you didn't even know *Claude* was his first name," Christian taunted as Carlos stood there looking stunned.

Suddenly going quiet and exchanging questioning glances, we all seemed to notice there was someone sitting in a dimly lit corner with their back to the rest of the room.

"What the fuck?" Christian asked under his breath.

"I know," I replied. "Who's that weirdo? Is that the owner?"

"How's it going?" Carlos asked a little too loudly.

No response.

"Would you like a drink?" Jaime asked. "We have a lot extra over here."

Christian started walking over. "Excuse me?" he said as he approached. "Excu— Oh, shit!"

"What? What is it?" asked Carolina, frightened.

"He's tied up. Help me get him out," Christian replied, flustered.

He squirmed as much as he could with all his limbs strapped to the chair. His eyes widened, and his fingers splayed when he noticed us approaching.

As we got closer, we saw DO NOT REMOVE written on the duct tape that sealed his lips and a white envelope on his lap that had READ ME written on it.

"What the fuck is this, guys?" Maria asked. "Let's just go."

"One step ahead of you," said Carlos, turning toward the direction we'd come in from. Then he stopped short. "Where's the door?"

Taking two steps farther than he had, Carolina replied, "I thought it was over here too."

"Hold up," said Christian as he walked over. "It was like one of those secret door type designs on the way in. I didn't notice it close behind us, but it was right here." He started banging along the wall, looking for a hollow point. "Hey, hello! Let us out of here."

No response.

"Maybe there's something in that letter. Let's open it," I said.

"I don't think we should," said Jaime. "Let's just get the fuck out of here and call the cops."

"We don't have a choice, babe," I replied. "And are we really just going to ignore the fact that there's a terrified guy over there, tied up and duct-taped to a chair?"

We all reluctantly agreed we should at least read that letter and see what the guy in the chair could shed light on. Did he even know why he was there? Maybe he was in the same boat as us.

The six of us circled his chair, and I signaled to him that I was going to take off the duct tape on his mouth.

He nodded in agreement.

As soon as the tape was removed, he began emphatically pouring his heart out. He spoke for two minutes straight, barely stopping to take a breath or let any of us slip a word in. But it didn't matter. None of us understood a word of the language he was speaking, and he didn't speak a lick of English or Spanish.

Carlos reached down and tugged on the zip ties binding his hands behind his back and to the seat, but no luck.

"Wait, should we be trying to untie him?" asked Carolina.

"What do you mean?" asked Jaime. "Of course we should."

"Wait, she's got a point," I interjected. "What if he's dangerous or something?"

"He's tied to a chair and more scared of us than we are of him," Carlos replied.

"Calm down, calm down," replied Christian. "Let's read the letter to see if it says anything about who he is and then make a determination after."

I slid the paper out of the envelope and began reading out loud. "This man's name is Guojing Zahn. He is a black market trader specializing in arms deals, some of which are linked to terrorist acts, human trafficking, and a significant 18 percent of the poisonous fentanyl that has flooded the underground drug scene in the US."

"Woah," said Christian.

I took a beat and then continued reading. "These are your instructions. Behind the bar, you'll find an untraceable .38 caliber pistol with no serial number. Put a bullet in his head, and you'll be free to go. Do not worry about his body or cleaning up. Those inconvenient logistics will be taken care of for you."

"This has to be some sick prank," Jaime said. "This can't be happening right now."

"We are not killing someone, guys," said Maria. "That's fucking murder!"

"Of course we're not," I replied. "Let's get the fuck out of here."

For the next several minutes, we fervently looked for a way out and, as a looming sense of hopelessness approached after our efforts proved futile, a projector screen came down in front of the bar area. The man who appeared introduced himself as Mr. Shinto's executive assistant. We could speak back to him, and he would hear us. However, after a cacophony of cuss words were lobbed at him like water balloons, he did most of the talking.

"Your instruction here tonight is simple," he started. "A simple task that carried out by any of you will result in the freeing of all of you."

"Why don't you do it yourself, you twisted fuck?" Carlos blurted out.

"Your moral apprehensions should not be a factor here, Mr. Rivera. I assure you that my employer does not want to bring harm to any of you. He simply wants the world to be rid of this vile individual."

"Wait, how the fuck do you know my name?" Carlos replied.

"We know each of your names, Mr. Rivera, as well as your recent whereabouts and who your closest friends and family are. Like your mother, living on 111th Street in Queens. Or your grandfather, Charles, Mrs. Ortega." He locked eyes with me and said, "Cousin Teresita." Then he continued, "The fact of the matter is that my employer has dedicated time and resources to making sure this happens properly and precisely as instructed. I assure you that no harm will come to you or your loved ones as long as you comply with the ask. Make no qualms about it, there's one way out of here. He leaves this world, and you get to leave this room."

"Why should we believe you, huh?" I shouted at the screen. "What if we don't do shit and just wait it out?"

"You see those six empty shot glasses sitting under those spouts? After one of you decides to stop dragging their feet and pulls the trigger, they will be filled with the last drink each of you will have tonight. Think of it as a celebratory toast of sorts."

"One, who said we would comply," replied Jaime. "And two, why would we drink some mysterious shot that might be cyanide or something that'll just kill us and keep us from going to the cops?"

"I assure you they're not poison, dear. Funny you should say that, though. Because they are the only thing that will counteract the slow-release poison each of you has *already* consumed."

"What the fuck? What poison?" asked Christian.

"The free rounds of drinks you've been enjoying, Mr. Torres. From the first sip each of you consumed, a slow acting but 100 percent deadly amount of arsenic trioxide has been coursing through you. In precisely one hour post consumption, your hearts will gradually grind down to a near halt. Your airways will constrict by an unsustainable 50 percent, at which point the most durable of you may live for an excruciatingly uncomfortable extra fifteen minutes or so. Unless, of course, you complete the task at hand, at which point the antidote to the poison surging through your bloodstreams will pour into those six shot glasses."

We stood there in absolute shocked silence.

"And with that, I trust the necessary motivation has been provided for you to fulfill my employer's ask. Oh, and in case you were wondering, your first sips were about forty-five minutes ago, giving you just shy of fifteen minutes to decide."

The screen went blank, the silence suddenly so loud it stunned us into motion.

"Where the fuck is that gun?" Carlos asked as he started toward the bar.

"Yea, I think he said it's back there," added Carolina as she followed behind.

"Wait, you guys," Jaime said. "What if it's bullshit? What if there is no poison?"

"If you want to stick around and find out, by all means. Me, I'm down to put this sex trafficking, drug poisoning fuck out of his misery," said Carlos.

The cold steel of the pistol somehow felt colder than the task at hand as he gripped it. While Carlos familiarized himself with the unfamiliar, those of us who said little else that night quietly agreed. But in that moment of silent despair, our lives were altered forever.

TRUE TO HIS WORD, once the lifeless body of Guojing Zahn slumped over in the chair and his blood pooled onto the ground, the antidote to the poison poured out of the spouts and into the shot glasses. Each of us drank one exactly as you'd imagine, as if our lives depended on it. Then a unique set of doors appeared after an entire wall slid open to show a long, narrow hallway leading out to the street.

"Follow me back to my place so we can figure this thing out," I told the guys.

"Your place?" exclaimed Maria. "Shouldn't we be heading to the nearest precinct or hospital or something?"

"To tell them what? That a guy on a projector made us kill someone after we self-administered poison?" I replied.

"He has a point," Jaime agreed. "I don't like it either, but he has a point. If this guy is as connected as he seems, who knows who he has paid off and how high his influence goes? If we rat him out, we'll be tied to chairs next."

"Honestly, I wasn't even thinking about that," I added. "But that's a good point. Let's go to my place and find out as much as we can about this son of a bitch."

That night was a wash. None of us could really think straight. The bit of research we were able to cobble together between meltdowns yielded no tangible results. All of us were in shock and filled with uncertainty and doubt about our futures. But in the days and weeks to come, that all faded away, only to be replaced by a deliberate resentment that fueled us. We needed to know who this man was, why he'd used us that way.

It took some doing, but we came to find out who the owner of the restaurant was, Hiroto Shinto, though he had hidden it well. Through my contacts at the registrar's office and some dots that Jaime connected by leveraging her law firm, we were able to trace the LLC from one shell company to the next until the eventual parent company listed him as the sole beneficiary and principal. A few of his companies had accounts registered at Christian's bank. With that, we got a glimpse of how deep his pockets were. His routine deposits were as consistent as a government check. Maria was an attorney at the DA's office and had many law enforcement and judicial relationships, which tipped her off to all the characters he allegedly conducted business with. He was spinning so many plates in both the legal and illegal arenas that it oddly warranted appreciation. Shinto was a boss in every sense of the word. If he wasn't directly involved with something, one or more of his subsidiaries were facilitating on some level. This guy was the connective tissue that stitched together every unsavory transaction in this town. He did business with the Italian and the Irish mobs. The shot callers of every major street gang like the Bloods, Latin Kings, Crips, and even a few biker gangs had some sort of dealing with him as well. He was a personification of the Silk Road. He facilitated money laundering, drug dealing, tax evasion schemes, murder for hire, and so much more. You name it, he did it or knew a guy or gal who did.

As time went on, it sank in. The more untouchable he became, the more our chances of holding him accountable diminished. Most of us began giving up our hopes for vigilante justice as the days became weeks and our joint research and brainstorming sessions grew fewer and farther between.

Carlos and Maria became fanatical about the guy for months after what happened, keeping tabs on his whereabouts, including events and functions he'd attend. They traced political contributions and the favors that were reciprocated. It became too much for Maria and she eventually let it go, but it wasn't as easy for Carlos. It put such a strain on their relationship that to this day there's a palpable tension betwixt them. That's based on how Jaime sees it, anyway. She still spoke with Maria every few weeks or so, though the rest of us drifted further apart. I think it made it easier to cope, not seeing or talking to each other. One less reminder of that night out.

Then one day, we all got the call.

I remember it being a Friday night because Jaime and I were getting ready for our movie night at home. My phone rang, and it was Carlos.

"Hey, Carlos. What's up, bro? How are you?" I said.

"Ups and downs. You know how it goes, Benny. But thankfully more ups lately. How about you?"

"Same old, man. Day by day, you know? Getting ready to watch a flick with Jaime."

"Hopefully not one that she picked out or you're in for a long night," he joked.

"Thankfully it's my week to choose, so we're good there," I replied.

"Listen, I won't keep you. I just wanted to invite you both to my place on Sunday around one in the afternoon. I invited the others. We'll get some lunch, catch up, and there's something I need to speak to you all about," Carlos stated.

"This Sunday? Okay, cool, that should work. I'll speak to Jamie about it, and we'll be there," I replied.

Saturday was a blink. And I couldn't remember what movie we watched that night if I tried. The anticipation over what the meeting was going to be about was all consuming for me. For Jaime too. Once Sunday came and we caught up with everyone, we soon found that the others felt the same way. Carlos stood before us in his living room, and we gave him our undivided attention.

"First and foremost, I want to thank you all for coming," Carlos began. "It truly means a lot to me that even if we're not as close as we once were, I could still reach out and count on you. I hope each of you knows that I'd do the same for you in a heartbeat."

"Don't mention it, brother," I said. "It has been a

minute since we've all been together. So what's this all about, anyway?"

"I wanted to tell you that after that night, I spent months wanting to kill myself," Carlos said. "I kept dreaming about how Guojing's blood spattered on the wall and pooled up on the floor. How that putrid stench of death danced with the smell of blood and bowl movements. And I swear that if it wasn't for the fear of how God was going to judge me for what I did that night, I would have gone through with offing myself."

"He was a horrible guy," I interjected. "We verified it ourselves. Everything that asshole told us he was, he was."

"Yea, you can't beat yourself up like that," Christian added. "You had no choice. We had no choice."

"I know," replied Carlos, "but it still weighs on me. And I know it must be weighing on you guys as well. It has been borderline unbearable, but knowing that untouchable cocksucker is out there has just compounded the entire experience into a crippling weight on my shoulders. What he did to us, he's probably done to half a dozen other people since then. Figuring out a way to get back at him has been my saving grace, and now we have a way to fight back. Now we can take that boulder-sized weight off our shoulders and crush the sonofabitch with it."

"How do you mean?" Maria asked as we were all thinking the same thing.

"He involved us all the day he lured and locked us in that room and drove us to kill Guojing," started Carlos. "It's going to take all of us to execute my plan and make things right."

"Carlos, are you speaking about going after this guy?" asked Maria. "Killing him? That's insane."

"Yea, bro. The guy is a piece of shit and God knows he

deserves it, but we're way over our heads," Christian added. "It'll be a suicide mission for sure."

"No," Carlos said sternly. "I'm saying that if we execute my plan with the requisite precision, we won't have to kill him. That part will work itself out."

We exchanged hesitant glances as we all processed and thought about it. Then we took a beat to separate into our couples and discuss it, but soon enough we huddled around Carlos and agreed to hear him out.

"So this is how it breaks down," Carlos began. "Five key members of separate crime organizations known as The Five Capos work with Shinto and are going to meet with an associate of his. We're going to break up that meeting and arrest the associate. He'll be taken in for questioning. The group doing the arresting and interrogating are part of a joint NYPD and FBI task force that not only owes Maria a few favors but also has a legit gripe with Shinto, his organization, and all of their own colleagues who are on the take. We expect those five shot callers to say they don't know Shinto or deny any involvement with him. The point is, though, that they're going to leave each of them with the seed of an idea that Shinto won't be paying them anymore because they got hemmed up."

"Okay, but won't that all fall apart when they continue to receive their payments?" asked Jaime.

"That's where phase two comes in," Carlos replied. "Each of those shot callers receives their payments from Shinto by way of money laundering. He takes the illegitimate dollars they make from selling the drugs he imports and pumps clean funds through their respective clean cash-heavy businesses like restaurants, laundromats, supermarkets, etc."

"The son of a bitch is getting paid on all sides," I said.

"Exactly," replied Carlos. "He imports and sells them the dope wholesale, then charges them a fee for laundering their profits."

"That's fucking ruthless," added Carolina.

"They're all criminals," Jaime chimed in as a reminder.

"Yea, they fancy themselves business executives," Carolina added. "You'd think they'd have a code."

"A code against greed?" asked Christian. "What business executive has that?"

"Yes, they're all businesspeople. Yes, they're all greedy. And yes, they're all criminals," Carlos said sternly. "All of that shit is inconsequential, though. We can and will use that information against them by fanning the flames of resentment that they'll already be feeling toward Shinto after they stop getting paid. What we want to do is plant the seed that the authorities know enough about the corruption to take him down. After that, the rest should fall into place."

"And how exactly are we supposed to do that?" I asked.

"They hold a quarterly meeting with that projector screen sidekick bitch. In person, in the same hotel suite, without fail. That's when we'll grab him. The task force is going to interrupt that meeting and take the sidekick out of there. But he'll undoubtedly have enough juice to get himself released within a couple of hours unless we have him taken to an undisclosed location," Carlos continued. "Either way, he's not the actual play. When the rest of them leave that hotel, we'll begin surveillance."

"We?" Carolina questioned.

"The task force," Carlos rebutted. "Given what they all saw happen the previous day, it won't be too farfetched for them to believe that the projector bitch began singing like a bird. What's even more important is that they'll *know* he wouldn't dime anyone out without Shinto's say so and that'll start them questioning the current structure of the regime."

"And I doubt these are the kind of men who take getting double-crossed lightly," said Jaime.

"Right," affirmed Carlos. "And that's exactly what we're counting on."

"I don't get it though," I stated. "What happens next? Won't they just sort out the misunderstanding like a *Three's Company* episode and move onto business as usual?"

"No. One of two things is going to happen," Carlos replied confidently. "Either the infighting causes a destabilization that will collapse their organization or..."

"Or what?" Christian asked after the pregnant pause.

"Or, they do Shinto the same way he made us take care of Guojing Zahn," Carlos replied. "It's a win-win, and don't think it's not. Do you guys think we're unique here? This is his MO. He coerces people into doing his dirty work while simultaneously compromising them so that he can leverage that shit in the future. You want to wait around for him to call in that favor? I sure as fuck don't."

"Damn, you remember his full name?" Carolina asked, surprised.

"How could I forget?" Carlos replied solemnly.

"You're making a lot of assumptions though, bro," I stated. "What if they move their meeting this quarter? What if the task force isn't able to take Projector Bitch while they're all watching? What if they get their money via some secondary fail safe that is already in place?"

"What if, what if, what if," Carlos mocked. "What if any of us could get a good night's sleep since that night? What if Maria didn't need to be hopped-up on Xanax just to function throughout the day? It's going to work. I know it is. But it's going to take all of us. Are you in or not?"

"I don't know about this, Carlos," replied Christian. "If things go wrong and any of these plans get out, I could lose my job over this shit."

"Your job?" Carlos replied. "Who got you the fucking job in the first place? Look," he continued after an awkward silence, "I wouldn't ask you to do any of this if it wasn't airtight. I wouldn't want you to jeopardize your job, for any of you. But I am asking you to put your trust in me because I've been meticulously crossing every t and dotting every i every day for almost a year now."

After about a minute of silent contemplation, Jaime chimed in with, "I wish I would've picked another restaurant that night."

That made us smile and ease up a bit. How could any of us not be in? We were in it however it was going to end. I mean, we were all already accomplices to murder. A forced murder that weighed in the favor of justice when balanced against the deeds Guojing Zahn committed, but it was still murder. A murder that required closure. Albeit for some of us more than others. The prospect of Shinto circling back to blackmail any one of us whenever he wanted was what solidified the choice for us though. And so we were in.

JUST SHY OF A WEEK LATER, Carlos's plan worked like a charm, you might say. Everything he said would happen, did. It couldn't have gone any smoother if the whole thing was scripted. The task force posted up on all four corners of the Losmina Inn hotel and had their surveillance van running point right across the street from the entrance. The Five

Capos pulled up as expected and were matched up to their surveillance photos. They arrived in close succession to one another, each in a fancier car than the last. Each with one to two body guards a piece. Shinto's right-hand showed up alone. Before moving in, the task force waited about twenty minutes so that the meeting would be underway. The lookout security guard they left in the lobby was isolated and cuffed first, before he could alert the others. A copy of the room key was procured at the front desk.

"I don't know which guests you're referring to, sir," the concierge said.

"You see this?" the officer replied while flashing his badge. "This means I can break down every door in this place until I find who I'm looking for. And you can explain to your boss why you interfered with official police business and why he now has dozens of broken doors to repair."

"Oh, you meant the penthouse meeting room. I'm terribly sorry I misunderstood your question. Let me get you a copy of the room key," he replied obligingly.

The first unit moved up to the penthouse suite expecting a bodyguard after seeing him on a monitor in the lobby and quickly neutralized him by the elevators. They proceeded toward the suite door, slid the keycard, and tactically let themselves in, weapons drawn.

"Nope, you won't be needing that," one officer said as he disarmed a guard on the inside of the door.

"I'll take that," another officer stated as she disarmed another.

"Gentleman, I assure you this is not a violent visit. It is a simple extraction mission," Officer Johnson stated as he scanned the room. "You," he said as he pointed to Shinto's right-hand man, "come over here."

"What is this about?" he replied nervously as he complied, walking tentatively in their direction.

"We'll discuss that downtown," the arresting officer replied.

"You're making a grave mistake. Do you know who I am?" he replied.

"We know exactly who you are, shit bird. Tell Shinto you're not coming home tonight," Officer Johnson interjected.

All the men in the room looked at each other nervously at the mention of his name.

"I assure you all this is a misunderstanding," Shinto's right-hand told them as the officers took him out of the room.

Right before stepping out himself, Officer Johnson turned back to the group and sarcastically said, "I wouldn't count on him coming back anytime soon, gentlemen. You know, the cloth he's cut from and all."

The arresting officers pressed forward as planned and drove Shinto's right-hand away. It didn't take long for each of The Five Capos to leave, but not before the surveillance crew had enough time to stash GPS trackers on each of their vehicles.

Across town, in a windowless ten by ten room, Shinto's right-hand sat with one hand cuffed to a cold metal table for twenty minutes before two officers walked in. He immediately blurted out, "I want my attorney!"

"You think we give a shit what you want? You think you get to run around doing what you do and still keep your fucking rights?" Officer Bustamante replied.

"Easy there," Officer Johnson said to his partner, balancing out the tension.

"Easy?" Officer Bustamante replied. "You know damn

well that this son of a bitch deserves nothing resembling easy."

"I assure you I've done nothing wrong. I furthermore assure you that I do have rights, good sir," Shinto's right-hand rebutted.

"The fuck you do," Officer Bustamante defied.

"Be that as it may," Officer Johnson continued. "We arrested you while in the presence of known kingpins, each with a rap sheet long enough to cover you up from head to toe...twice. Each one of them is personally responsible for at least half a dozen murders, and their crews can be attributed with a dozen more easily. You have no identification on you. You won't tell us your name. Can you please at least explain to us what you were doing there?"

"I don't think I'm making myself clear, Officers," he replied. "I do not belong here. And I want my lawyer to help make that make sense to you."

"Fine. If you insist, let's see how it plays out," he replied. Then he and Officer Bustamante turned away and started for the door.

Officer Johnson turned back and said, "Tell me something though, Mr. Ocampo, how long is it going to take your attorney to get here if we've only been able to get in touch with his office answering service?"

"And you know we can't leave sensitive information like this with a third party," Officer Bustamante added.

Hearing that they knew his real name wiped the smug look off the executive assistant's face immediately.

Officer Johnson closed the door and let him stew a while longer.

Meanwhile, two surveillance units tracked the GPSs coordinates of the capos' vehicles and noted that they were headed to a specific rendezvous point, so they headed that way as well. They posted up with binoculars and a tele-photo lens camera in hand. The Italian and the Irish mob capos showed up first, followed by the Bloods, Latin Kings, and Crip Shot Callers. They couldn't get in close enough to make out any of their conversations, but their body language seemed to echo their frustrations and concerns about Mr. Ocampo giving them up to save his own ass. They left after about ten minutes, nothing seeming any more or less settled. They were definitely frazzled though, stated each unit as they reported back to Johnson and Bustamante.

"Any word on Shinto?" Johnson asked.

"Negative," Agent Santos replied.

"We'll smoke him out," Johnson said. "His accounts get frozen at 0800. Once those dry up, a lot of people are going to start looking for him. It'll behoove him to keep the temperature on the streets cool."

THE SIX OF us all met up that evening at Christian's apartment to prep for the next day. Officer Johnson came by to let us know he was still holding Mr. Ocampo at an undis-closed location, but they had to cut him loose soon.

"Can you keep him a bit longer?" Carlos asked.

"What's a bit longer?" Johnson replied.

"Two to three days," answered Carlos.

"Two to three days?! Are you nuts?" Johnson replied. "I was thinking two to three more *hours*. We're damn near kidnapping the guy as is."

"No, you're *absolutely* kidnapping the guy as is," inter-jected Jaime.

"Don't waver now," Carlos rebutted. "The brass of a

crime family that is responsible for untold tons of smuggled drugs and countless murders will not prioritize ratting you out for kidnapping one of them."

"We'll stretch for two more days," replied Officer Johnson. "After that...well, I hope you have a Plan B."

Christian went to work the next day, nervously making an effort to get through his usual routines like normal. As he rode on the subway, he ordered his usual two breakfast wraps and large coffee with almond milk, no sugar, via the app on his phone. Picking them up on the way, he then walked the half block to his office building.

Smiling, he greeted the security guard like he always did. "Hey, Fred," he said as he walked through the turnstile after scanning his ID card. "Tough loss last night, wasn't it?"

"Mr. Torres," Fred replied along with a hat tip in his direction. "They just don't play defense, man. And don't get me started on the coaching staff."

When he finally settled at his desk, he reached in his pocket and pulled out a small sheet of paper that had been folded in half. He unfolded it to reveal each of Shinto's account numbers. He used the account numbers to plug them into an SQL code that would flag and freeze all the accounts for a mandatory thirty days while a suspected terrorist investigation took place. The SQL also masked his user ID from showing up in the audit trail. Then he sat back, sipped on his coffee, and ate his breakfast.

The task force grew impatient as the hours pressed on. They were holding Mr. Ocampo at a nearby warehouse, while continuing to surveille the members of The Five Capos. Still no signs of Shinto, but with his money dried up and his mouthpiece temporarily out of the picture, unable to answer questions, The Five Capos were plotting a coup of his organization.

While on surveillance duty, Officer Childress turned to his partner and asked, "Can you believe these mopes?"

"What do you mean?" she replied.

"These mopes," he continued. "They're part of one of the most successful and entrenched crime organizations we've ever seen, and at the first sign of instability, they're looking to overthrow the boss and take over shit."

"Power vacuums, man," she replied. "You take out a major player and the remaining ones get sucked into that void and come out of the other side with asinine plots and plans."

"Fuckin' ingrates is what they are," he replied.

"That's a weird way to look at it," she said.

"How do you mean?" Childress replied.

"Well, for starters, you're acting as if these are normal people," she began. "They're not law-abiding citizens who operate with logic and reason. They're sociopaths that on a good day weigh their crime options against their risk tolerance. They'll do anything for financial gain. Psychopathic killers that don't skip a beat between ordering dinner and ordering a hit. Being grateful for anything isn't an emotion I'd expect any of them to even be capable of, let alone show."

"Fair point, Robertson," Childress replied. "Fair point."

That's when the call came in.

"Look, look, something's happening. I think he's calling them," Robertson said.

"What? Who?" replied Childress. "Shinto?"

"Yes, just look at the one on the phone," she said.

"Yea, so?" replied Childress.

"He's shutting the rest of them up while he talks. What do you think that's about?" she said.

"Maybe it's his wife or something," Childress replied.

"Not everyone is as chicken shit scared of their lady as you are," Robertson said. "Let's see what they do after this."

The group dispersed after the call, each of their cars being tracked to the Losmina Inn hotel where they reconvened. Whoever was on the other end of that phone call must've setup this meet. The expectation was that Shinto himself would show up to ease the tension on the street.

"Hit up the others," Robertson told Childress. "Tell them to meet us at the hotel. Shit's about to get real."

"Copy that," he replied.

Within minutes the teams were in motion and closing in on the hotel. They secured the perimeter a couple blocks away and stealthily approached. Each team took up the same positions as last time, but on three of the four corners since Officers Johnson and Bustamante were still babysitting Mr. Ocampo. Childress and Robertson covered the front entrance, having accounted for each of The Five Capos and their security details. The thing was, they didn't know what to look for when it came to Shinto. He was a ghost. Legend had him being anywhere from five-foot-nothing to eight feet tall and everything in between. No one had ever dealt with him directly. There was always a go-between like Mr. Ocampo. The only constant in his descriptions was a large red birthmark that took up a quarter of his face. It was said to be so prominent that it tinted his left eye a reddish hue. It had taken some less than pleasant coercion for Johnson and Bustamante to get a description of Shinto out of Ocampo, and then they really didn't know how much of it, if any, they could trust, but it was all they had to go on.

An hour later, still nothing.

"How many did we say went in there?" Officer Robertson asked.

"Twelve," replied Officer Childress.

"I'm counting fifteen," Robertson replied.

"What? Let me see," Childress stated as he looked through the binoculars and counted for himself. "Son of a bitch. How'd he get past us?"

"Call it in to the rest," Robertson said.

"Copy." And he did.

"What's the game plan?" Childress asked. "Just wait until the fucker comes out?"

"No, we can't wait on him to come out if we don't even know how he got in," replied Robertson. "We have to get inside and near that room."

"And do so without tipping off the staff," replied Officer Childress. "There's no telling who's on the take and able to tip him off."

"I'll do it," said Robertson. "But I need you to be my eyes up here, and two units need to go in and cause a front desk distraction so that I can get by them unnoticed. Do we have a confirm on the room number?"

"It's the penthouse, P2100," replied Agent Flores via their two-way communication. "There are three other rooms on the same floor, so you don't have to worry about it being a private single entrance off the elevator."

Robertson made her way to the hotel bar adjacent to the front desk. Agents Flores and Santos walked up to the front desk attendant and demanded money back from a supposed previous stay. While they were busy distracting him, Robertson nonchalantly slid toward the elevator bank. She grabbed a nearby service cart and took it with her. The entire team was in plain clothes, so tying her sweater around her waist and putting on a name tag she found on the cart would help her blend into the background. She hung around an adjacent penthouse entrance, fussing with the service cart as if she worked there while reporting back to the team outside. They advised Shinto was still in there, holding court.

When the meeting broke and the crews began exiting, they didn't pay her any extra attention. She kept a mental tally of each member leaving and accounted for each shot caller and crew. All twelve. All except Shinto. Once the hallway and elevator banks cleared, she quietly reported back to the team outside. They continued to surveil the room, confirming he was still there along with two other individuals.

"Let us know when he heads to the elevators and we'll take him as soon as he steps foot into the lobby," said Childress.

"Copy," Robertson replied.

Shinto and his crew never came out into the hallway, though. After surveillance reported no one within their view for twenty minutes, Robertson knocked on the door under the guise of housekeeping.

There was no answer.

"Do you see anyone on your end?" she asked.

"No, they must still be in that other room opposite the window," Childress replied.

"Robertson, I have an idea," Agent Flores chimed in from the lobby with Agent Santos. "Sit tight for ten minutes."

After making a fuss to speak to management about their reimbursements and even getting the regional manager on the phone to help sort out the mess, Agent Santos reengaged the front desk concierge and asked if there was anywhere they could speak privately, away from all the strangers in the lobby, so that they could sort this out. To quell the negative vibes, the concierge obliged and took Agent Santos to his office. In doing so, Agent Flores was able to slip behind the desk and begin navigating the hotel keycard system.

"Robertson, you still with me?" Agent Flores asked about four minutes later.

"Yea, still no sign of Shinto," she replied.

"I'm coming up," said Agent Flores.

"What's the plan?" she asked when he came off the elevator.

"I have the keycard. I'll swipe you in and cover you. But keep up the housekeeping routine and be ready for anything. Agent Santos will wait for us in the lobby, and the team outside will stay posted. Everyone copy?"

"Copy," said Officer Childress.

"Copy," said Agent Moledo.

"Roger that," said Agent Sterling.

"Copy," Agent Santos replied shortly after wrapping things up with the concierge.

"Hello, housekeeping," Robertson said as Flores swiped the card and tentatively turned the door handle. Then she repeated it a few seconds later while they the two crept through the door.

They went about searching the penthouse, finding nothing.

"It's empty," Agent Flores reported.

"How's that?" said Childress. "What do you mean, empty? It can't be empty."

"John," Robertson replied, addressing Childress, "he's not here. We've looked everywhere."

"No, that can't be. He has to be there. Look for another

way out, a laundry chute...something!" Childress replied franticly.

Flores and Robertson scanned the walls in the room that Shinto and the crew had gone into, knocking on them, searching for a hollow sound that might indicate a secret passageway or hidden door.

Sure enough, they found it. The walk-in closet had a false back wall. Pulling down on the rod made it slide open, exposing a direct entrance to the next penthouse apartment. It was filled with surveillance equipment and monitors that showed every inch of the original apartment where all meetings were held.

Robertson called it in. "We cleared the apartment and found a secret door adjoining two of the penthouses. That's how he could slip in and out undetected."

"But don't they all lead to the same hallway and elevator vestibule? None of us have seen them come out the building, past any windows, nothing," Childress said.

"This one's empty too," said Agent Flores. "There has to be a separate way out of this apartment."

They opened up door after door, closet after closet, and searched for another hollow wall in the back rooms of the suite. Nothing. Until they opened up the double door to the master bedroom and revealed a freight elevator.

"Holy shit," said Robertson.

"What? What is it?" replied Childress.

"There's a fucking freight elevator in this apartment," she replied.

"What? That's not in the building plans," Moledo chimed in.

"We're taking it down to see where it leads," Robertson replied.

"Moledo and Childress, meet us on the north side of the

building for backup and keep your eyes peeled in case you see Shinto and his crew still around," said Flores.

"Copy," replied Moledo.

"We're on it, boss," replied Childress.

Officer Robertson and Agent Flores went into the freight elevator and pressed the singular down button.

"You ready?" Flores asked as he drew his sidearm.

"Ready," Robertson confirmed as she did the same.

The freight lift jerked to a stop at the lower level and the doors opened. Officer Robertson and Agent Flores stepped out slowly, guns drawn, and began quietly securing the perimeter of the private indoor parking garage before them.

Flores signaled Robertson to stop, indicating he had heard something. They quietly listened to a faint conversation carrying on in the distance while peeking around a concrete pillar.

There was Shinto, having a stern conversation on his cellphone while instructing his guards to prepare to get going. Silhouettes of the two guards he was with were visible through the rear tinted window of the SUV, which was facing a closed garage door.

Robertson called it in. "They're still here. Repeat, still here. Circle to the southwest part of the building. Look for a closed steel garage door that will probably open up to a remote area."

"There's an alleyway on the south side," Flores whispered.

"Look for an alleyway," Robertson echoed on the call. "Do not, I repeat, do not let the black SUV leave the premises. Our three suspects are all here and all considered armed and dangerous, so take all the necessary precautions. Shinto is the shorter one, and we need him alive. I repeat, Shinto is the shorter of the three and we need him alive. We will flank from behind once they make a move, so pause your fire unless absolutely vital."

With that, Agent Flores and Officer Robertson waited for Shinto to finish up his call and get in the SUV. Soon, Shinto got in the back seat of the SUV and closed the door as his driver triggered the garage door to rise. The exit was clear, and they drove out.

Then the wail of sirens echoed in through the open door as two vehicles raced in and slammed to a stop in front of Shinto's SUV, blocking them in right on time. The driver hit it in reverse almost instantly. There was only one way out, though.

"Police! Stop your vehicle. Shut off the engine, and throw the keys out the window," said Agent Santos over the loudspeaker.

"すぐに私たちをここから出してください," Shinto yelled. (Get us out of here right away!)

The driver put the vehicle in drive and punched it toward the exit, smashing into both task force vehicles. In anticipation of this reaction, there was still a driver behind the wheel of each police vehicle, and they sped up and rammed right back into the SUV, matching its force with an equal and opposite reaction.

They were at a standstill, and both the driver and passenger reached for their weapons. Before they could pull them out, however, Agent Flores and Officer Robertson swooped in.

"I wouldn't do that if I were you," Robertson said as she cocked her Glock 19 and aimed it at the front seat passenger's head through the window.

"Nuh-uh, I wouldn't try that if I were you," said Flores as he pressed the barrel of his gun against the driver's temple and stopped him in his tracks.

"くそ, what do I pay you for?!?" exclaimed Shinto. "Kill them now!"

"If you make any sudden movements, your brain's going to be splattered all over that nice jacket your buddy's wearing over there," said Flores to the driver.

Officer Childress and Agent Moledo moved in and opened the back door. "Mr. Shinto, you are under arrest," stated Childress. "Please step out of the vehicle, sir."

"Do you know who I am?" Shinto replied. "Who is your commanding officer? Call him right now."

"Sorry, this is more like overtime work for us," replied Childress. "No one's available to take your call at the moment."

"Ahh, I see. Who hired you?" asked Shinto. "I'll pay you ten times whatever they are."

"What? And ruin the fun?" replied Childress as he cuffed him and escorted him out.

"What do we do with these two?" asked Agent Moledo with a head nod toward the two goons in the front seat.

"Take their weapons," replied Robertson, "and put these on." She tossed him a pair of tie wraps. "We'll leave them in here and have a unit pass by to cut them loose tomorrow morning."

"Hey, wait, you can't do that," one of them exclaimed.

"Really?" replied Robertson. "You really think you have a say in the matter, motherfucker?"

"Let's go," she told Flores.

And so they went, Shinto shuffling along in between them with his hands zip-tied behind his back.

～

"WE HAVE Shinto in custody and we're on our way toward you," Robertson texted Officer Bustamante. "We'll be there in thirty minutes. Make sure they see each other when we walk in with him."

"Copy," Bustamante texted back.

They walked Shinto in, down a hallway toward a back room. On the way, they slowed down as they passed an open door and naturally everyone looked in. When Shinto did, he locked eyes with Mr. Ocampo, who had a sheet of paper with writing on it and a pen sitting on the table in front of him.

"Sir, I haven't told them—" a very flustered Mr. Ocampo began as Officer Johnson shut the room door closed.

Flores led Shinto into a room a few doors down. "Have a seat," he instructed.

"I want my lawyer," Shinto said sternly.

"Oh, you still don't get it, do you?" said Flores. "This isn't your typical situation. This is purely to show you that the untouchable *can* be touched."

"Fair enough," Shinto replied. "Ten million American dollars for you and your team to split up as you see fit."

"This isn't about money," Flores replied.

"Okay, fifty million," Shinto said defiantly.

"You can't buy your way out of this one, asshole," Robertson added.

He sat for a minute, trying to discern if these officers of the law were being earnest. "One hundred million," he stated emphatically, "wired to any account you want within twelve hours."

"Okay," replied Robertson, "now I'm just offended. What if we would have agreed to the ten million? Now I can't accept it out of principle alone." Sarcasm rang loud and clear in her tone.

"Besides," added Flores, "I thought you weren't able to wire any funds to anybody anymore?"

With that, the smug smirk he had on his face faded. His eyes widened and seemed to darken like a shark's. He slammed his free hand on the table while the other remained shackled to it. "Release my funds," he said defiantly, "or I'll see to it that even your grandchildren curse you for the day you ever crossed me."

In that moment, the door burst open. Officer Childress beelined to Shinto and walloped him across the face with the grip and magazine of his gun, instantly spraying Shinto's blood all over the table and floor.

"You done fucked up now," said Officer Robertson.

"Please, it's not me. The man you have in the other room is the leader. I am for show," Shinto pleaded surprisingly quickly.

"Funny," replied Childress. "That's not his tune. He sang like a canary and told us all about the ins and outs of your organization."

"Yup," said Agent Flores. "The cops you have on the take, the judges you helped get elected, politicians…those last two alone make this a big federal issue. The first one just pisses off good police like my officer buddy over here."

"It didn't take much at all to get him to speak either," Childress interjected before striking the man across the face again. "You must not treat your people very well."

"Shame on you, Shinto," added Robertson. "You should know better than that. If you don't feed your people, then after an inevitable amount of time, you become the main course."

"And your buddy in the other room has been on a feeding frenzy over the past few hours," said Childress. "He's been dishing on cats we didn't even know were in the mix."

"The signed testimony he gave us is enough to lock you up *under* a prison for life," Robertson added.

"What is it you want from me? Name your price," replied a defeated Shinto.

"For you to take a nap. A nice. Long. Nap," replied Agent Flores as he jabbed Shinto with a syringe in the upper right shoulder of the arm that was shackled.

Head spinning and eyes glazing over, Shinto slurred an incoherent sentence. Then he keeled forward and his head dropped onto the table.

Agent Flores made a call. "We're ready. Are you set up? Okay, we'll be there in twenty." Turning to Childress and Robertson, he said, "Let's go."

They picked Shinto's slumped over body up and headed out the door.

"How about Ocampo?" Robertson asked.

"After we leave, we'll have Johnson and Bustamante cut him loose," Agent Flores replied. "Tell him something like Shinto bribed us to let him go and that he thinks Ocampo gave up the entire organization. That'll be more than enough for him to skip town for good."

Shinto woke up in the same spot where Guojing Zahn had gasped his last breath. He struggled a bit before giving up in hopelessness. He looked over all of us, sitting there in the booth in front of him. Jaime and I, Carlos and Maria, Christian and Carolina...all of us sat staring back at the man, quite pleased that Carlos's plan had worked so flawlessly.

Agent Flores and Officers Robertson and Childress stood around behind Shinto.

"Who let you in here? Who are you?" said Shinto.

"The owner let us in," replied Carlos.

"I am the owner!" he replied defiantly.

"Not anymore. Actually, you never really were," said Jaime. "It's a funny thing when it comes to LLC shell companies and using someone with a clean name to be the owner on paper for all the storefront businesses. They can legally sell your shit."

"Or, in your case, give it away," added Christian. "But don't worry, you still own the parent company, though now it has no businesses left under it."

The projector screen came down with Mr. Ocampo on it again. But this time it was a recording from the interrogation room where Officers Bustamante and Johnson had been holding him.

Shinto's eyes widened as the gears in his head turned in realization of what had happened. The paperwork in front of Ocampo wasn't a signed confession. He'd been signing deed transfers.

"Yep," said Jaime. "We handed every one of your sixteen laundering companies over to The Five Capos. The restaurants, the warehouses, the laundromats, the shipping company, and the car dealerships. All of it. Gone."

"You see, what you called providing them with convenience by using your laundering and distribution services," said Carlos, "they saw for what it actually was. Price gouging them with fees. They formed a cooperative and now have a truce around that part of their business. Each of them gets to expand their territories, and they're still going to be making more money than they ever did with you. You're obsolete, chief."

"Greed, as it turns out, isn't that good after all," added Christian.

"You think you've covered everything, do you?" replied Shinto. "You think those savages can maintain the stability and consistency that I've put in place? The comforts that your colleagues in law enforcement and those self-serving politicians need to cushion their lives with?"

"Stability and consistency?" interjected Robertson. "The stability of your drug distribution and the consistency of unsolved John Doe murders are not the stability and consistency we're interested in here. We're restoring the natural order of things. Removing your cancerous ass from continuing to affect those within our ranks, so that we can get back to being real police again. Good police."

"And a truce, for however long that bullshit lasts, means less violence on my streets," said Childress. "So we win all around. You finally lose, fucko."

"Untie me," said Shinto defiantly, "or by this time next week, each of you will be investigating the disappearances of anyone you've ever cared about. You can each patiently wait for a break in the case as I mail pieces of their bodies to your homes week after week after week."

"Oh, you still haven't processed the gravity of the situation you're in, have you?" asked Flores. "Let me make this very clear to you. You will not see next week."

Shinto's eyes widened as Agent Flores and Officers Robertson and Childress walked out of the room. Five of us followed soon after, while Carlos stayed behind. If looks could kill, Shinto would have dropped dead right then and there, caught in Carlos's visual crosshairs. But he didn't, and Carlos walked away as the Latin King's capo made his way in and greeted Carlos warmly.

"Yo, what's up, B?" he said.

"Not much, Swifty. Damn, how long has it been, man?" replied Carlos.

"Since the funeral, I think, right?" Swifty replied. "So like four or five years."

"That's crazy, man. Time flies," said Carlos.

"I gotta tell you, B, when you first hit me up about this, I didn't think it would work," began Swifty. "But you always been a savvy dude. Everything is flowing like never before, and I want you to know that I'm thankful. We all are."

"Nah, bro, don't mention it," Carlos said.

"Seriously, if you ever need anything, you just hit me up. We owe you," Swifty affirmed.

"What you're doing for me now is more than enough," replied Carlos. "Trust me."

"Don't worry, B. I got you," said Swifty.

"Let me ask you something, though. You ever wonder how things would have been if Derek was still around?" asked Carlos.

"Shit, all the time. I wouldn't be doing this, that's for sure," Swifty replied. "He would have had us all setup lovely, making ends legit-like, you know?"

"You know you can still do it yourself, right? You ever think about leaving all this shit behind? Getting out alive? You got money. You can do it," replied Carlos.

"Nah, man, this is it for me," replied Swifty. "Wherever this road leads, I'm walking it. I made my peace with that a long time ago, B. And I appreciate the hookup here. I want you and your people to know that. Again, if you ever need anything, just say the word."

"Nah, man, thank you," replied Carlos. "We couldn't have pulled it off without you and your guys."

"You sure you don't want to come and let that thing go yourself? Get some closure?" asked Swifty.

"Nah, man, that's not me anymore," replied Carlos.

"You right, you right. Shit, to be honest, that wasn't you even when it was you. Don't worry about a thing," Swifty added. "We'll clean this all up real nice. Be safe, my guy."

"Thanks, bro," replied Carlos as he gave Swifty a pound. "You too."

Carlos walked toward that long corridor he hadn't seen since the night with Guojing Zahn as Swifty executed the last piece of the elaborate plan. Walking up behind Shinto, he fired two rounds into the back of his head. The shots echoed throughout the corridor and blended into the sounds of the city at the same moment that Carlos stepped foot outside, took a deep breath, and sighed in relief.

"We don't have a choice." That's what I'd told Jaime when she'd said we should have gotten the fuck out of there and called the cops in the very beginning of all this. "We don't have a choice."

Thinking back on those frantic moments leading up to that trigger being pulled though, I wonder. It made me question the fragility of it all. How effortless it could be to tug on the loose ends of the fabric of society. How quickly things can unravel. When your back is to the wall and you're coerced at a moment where being between a rock and a hard place seems like an improvement of circumstances. Right then, decisions truly are life changing.

PENCIL CASE

Remember that period of time before school started again? When summer vacation was almost over and the excitement of getting new school supplies temporarily drowned out memories of having to do too much homework instead of watching Power Rangers, VR Troopers, or Batman (the animated series, not the Adam West reruns, although I'd have an affinity for those a bit later in life)?

There was this one summer between second and third grade when I used to go with my dad to the supermarket where he worked. He managed the deli and opened up the place way before he actually needed to be there. To him, being punctual meant being somewhere an hour or two before you were expected. You know, in case you got a flat tire on the way, or your car exploded, so you could get it fixed and still be on time to handle your responsibilities.

I didn't mind getting up early with him, though. Excited about going to work with my dad, my seven-year-old brain was so jacked up I barely slept the night before anyway. I'd wake up, brush my teeth, get dressed, and be ready to leave on time. We'd drive the ten to fifteen minutes it took to get there and open up shop.

This one morning, the two dudes who worked as shelf stockers were already out front, sipping on their fifty-cent cart coffees. Not my pop though. He got his Bustelo out of the way at home. Mom prepared it for him the night before, and he brewed it before the sun came up. He had it along with a piece of Entenmann's butter loaf pound cake, while he listened to either 1010 WINS or Radio WADO 1280 on the AM radio dial.

He said, "What's up," to the guys, who seemed happy to see him and patted me on the head.

"*¿Quien es este chikiyo?*" one of them said, asking who I was.

"*Este es el hijo mas pequeño mio,*" my pop responded, introducing me as his youngest. "*Saludalo a Ramón,* Tony," he instructed me.

"*Hola,*" I said timidly.

"*Pero con la voz alata, para que te pueda oir,*" Dad added, "*y dale la mano.*" He'd always get on me about greeting etiquette and speaking clearly.

"*Hola,*" I said a bit louder as I shook Ramón's hand.

"*¿O, se llama Tony tambien?* We're going to call you Tony Junior, *para no confundirnos. ¿Vas a trabajar con tu papi?*" he asked.

"*Sí,*" I responded.

"*Que bueno,*" he said, "That's good," he added in broken English.

My dad and the other guy, who I would later come to know as Miguel, rolled up the metal gate in front of the supermarket, and then my dad went in alone to shut off the alarm and flick on the lights. He was the only one the owners trusted with the keys and alarm code. I stayed outside with Ramón and Miguel for a bit, until all the lights came on.

To this day, I still remember walking in for the first time. I mean, I've been in supermarkets before, this one in particular a couple times while it was bustling with shoppers and workers. But being the first ones through the door, watching the lights go on, felt like I was in on a secret. I was privy to the behind-the-scenes of how this place transitioned every night from dormant to lively.

We walked past the cashier stations and around the lotto station, which I later learned was where the owner hung out at so he could keep his eye on the money and cashiers. We made our way to the deli in the back-right corner from where we were standing. Dad flicked on the light switches to the display fridges where the cold cuts and cold salads were, while I roamed around his workspace, his work domain, excited to be on this side with an opportunity to see how the sausage was made. There were notepads and scraps of paper sitting on a small table. Others hung with magnets on the side of the standing fridge. All seemed to be lists of different deli meats.

Soon after, Dad washed his hands thoroughly and put on an apron he had hung up on a hook the day before.

"*Vamos a buscar el pan,*" he told me.

There's nothing particularly thrilling about getting bread, I thought, but I was excited to be embarking on our first official work task. "*¿El pan?*" I asked, surprised to hear there was more.

"*Sí, tengamos que hacer el pan fresco cada día,*" he replied, expounding on the fact that he also baked bread daily.

With that, we went up one aisle toward the back of the supermarket. My eyes scanned around in awe like I hadn't seen a cereal aisle before, while I tried to keep up with my dad's speed walking. There was a double door with an Employees Only sign, and he pushed through them like he owned the place.

"*Ven por aquí*," he instructed, "*ten cuidado con las escaleras*," he warned while we walked down a dimly lit, jagged staircase.

We walked down a dingy flight of stairs, into a poorly lit basement filled with broken down cardboard boxes and cases of the products that would eventually fill the shelves of the aisles upstairs. Ramón and Miguel were hard at work lifting cases, breaking down boxes and then tying them up, and sending cases of goods up a flat escalator looking thing to be stocked on the shelves upstairs.

"*¿Cómo va eso, muchachos?*" Dad asked, greeting the same guys we saw earlier.

"Hey, Tony *y* Tony Junior," Ramón replied as he continued on with his work.

Dad opened up a walk-in box refrigerator and grabbed a big bag filled with frozen dough-like cylinders, and he gave me a slightly smaller one to carry.

"*¿Tú puedes con esa?*" he asked to check if I could handle the weight of it.

"*Sí,*" I responded quickly to not let him down, but I wasn't so sure that I could carry it. I lifted the bag awkwardly in front of me with both hands and followed him back the way we came.

"*¿Tony, vio el juego de los Mets anoche?*" Miguel asked.

"*Si, que barbaridad. No tienen pitcheo. Sin pitcheo mejor no van para parte ellos,*" my dad responded as Miguel nodded in agreement about the Mets not having solid enough pitching.

"*Nos vemos en lonche, muchachos,*" Dad added as we went back up the dingy staircase.

When we made it back to the deli, he cranked up one of the two long ovens to a specific temperature he had marked on the knob with black permanent marker because the actual numbers had rubbed off already. Then he reached into his right pocket and pulled out a pocketknife that he used to slice open both the bags we'd brought up. He put down three flat trays and instructed me to pass him the bread. "Okay, *empieza a pasarme el pan*."

I went into the bag and began handing them over to him quickly. "*¿Por qué están tan duros?*" I asked. I'd never seen hard, icy bread before.

"*Porque tengamos que cocinarlo todavía*," he clarified, "*estas son la masa del pan y las congelamos para que no se dañen antes de cocinarlas. Vamos, más rápido, papi*," he instructed, and I picked up the pace accordingly.

Once they were all on trays, he pulled out a Windex-looking spray bottle that had a clear liquid in it and began spraying the first tray of bread.

"*¿Que es eso?*" I asked, wondering what it was.

"*Agua*," he responded. "*Para que se cocinen bien. Tóma, échale a los otros*," he told me as he handed over the bottle while he grabbed and slid the completed tray into the oven.

I began spraying, and after a bit he said, "*No lo mojes tanto. Y házlo más rápido, papi.*"

I tried doing it as fast as I could but started losing grip strength after about half a dozen rolls.

He took the bottle and said, "*Ven para ayudarte*," and sprayed each roll from both remaining trays precisely three times each, faster than the machine gun from *Contra*. He put the still-frozen dough in the oven. Through the oven window, I could see that as the frost melted, cold condensation evaporated almost instantly. "Okay," he said, "*Vamos a sazonar los pollos y ya estaremos listo para cuando abran el supermercado.*"

"*¿Tu haces pollos también?*" I asked, and he nodded in agreement. He baked bread, seasoned and cooked rotisserie chickens, and made sure the deli was fully stocked before the supermarket even opened. My pops was Superman. The sun slept in longer than he did. He ran the deli in a supermarket where he was also the most trusted employee. He made bread, shot the shit with his coworkers that obviously liked him, and made whole chickens that I saw him season, marinate, and slide onto spinning metal spits five at a time. Then he put them into an oven that I now knew was the culprit behind a few burn-mark scars he had on his hands and forearms. He worked through lunch every single day, and he serviced every single one of his customers with a smile regardless of if he was sick that day or in a shitty mood. In retrospect, I realize I internalized those traits and attempt to replicate that type of work ethic and discipline in my own life.

"*¿Tienes hambre?*" he asked me around lunchtime.

I said no based on his body language, not looking like he was letting up anytime soon, and I didn't want him to think any less of me for wanting to take a break. I was hungry, though.

"*Tienes que comer algo, mi hijo, te voy hacer un sándwich. ¿Con que lo quieres? Elige lo que quieras,*" he said as he pointed to all the cold cuts I could choose from.

My brain filled up with combination ideas as my eyes glazed over all the options—ham, honey ham, Muenster cheese, turkey, salami, bologna.

My dad offered a suggestion after seeing my indecision. "*¿Lo quieres con jamón y queso?*"

"*No, no jamón,*" I replied.

"*¿Y bologna?*" he offered. "*A ti te gusta eso.*"

"*No, tampoco quiero eso,*" I replied indecisively.

Ultimately, I settled on a buttered roll with American cheese. To this day, it was the best sandwich I've ever had. I shit you not. I don't know what it was. Maybe the fresh, warm roll contrasting with the cold cheese and creamy butter. Maybe it was the love my dad put into it. Whatever it was, I haven't had one that good since.

This lady walked by and behind the deli where we were.

"*Hola, Carmen, ven a conocer a mi hijo,*" my dad told her, inviting her to meet me.

"*Saludo,*" she responded. "*¿Oh este es el Tony Jr.? ¿Este es el grande o el pequeño? ¿Tienes dos, no?*"

"*El pequeño,*" my dad replied.

"*Si ya estas vuelto un hombre,*" she said. "*Hola, papito. Yo soy Carmen, la amiga de tú papi,*" she stated as she leaned over to introduce herself.

"*Hola, Carmen,*" I said, loud enough this time. Then I bit into the last quarter of my sandwich. I love that my dad cut it into fours. Maybe that's what made it taste better. It made the sandwich last longer for sure.

"*¿Tony, que hai de bueno hoy?*" Tengo hambre.

"*Bueno, le puedo hacer un sándwich,*" my dad told her.

Good choice, I thought to myself.

"*O le preparo una ensaladilta de papa con pollo, cuando esten listo,*" he added as an option.

"*No, no quiero nada de eso hoy,*" Carmen replied. "*Voy a ir a los chinitos del lado a comprar una sopa. ¿Quieres una?*"

"*No, no, ya yo comí,*" my dad said even though he hadn't eaten.

He was just telling her that so he could get back to focusing on work. He never ate lunch. Instead, he worked straight through and ate a big meal when he got home. My mom would have a spread prepared for him every day as he walked in around 2:30 to 3:00 p.m. sharp. A mixed salad, a plate of rice, a bowl of beans, and a plate of a protein like *pollo al horno* or *bistec encebollado*. Sometimes *tostones* too, if *plátanos* were on sale that week and we had some left over from weekend breakfasts.

"Okay, *después vengo a buscar a Tonito junior para que empaque y se haga unos chavitos*," Carmen said as she walked away. "*Nos vemos.*"

I was about to ask my dad what she meant by taking me with her to go pack, but he had a couple customers waiting and the attention span of a seven-year-old is not far off from that of a goldfish.

After he finished giving them what they asked for, my dad pulled out two rolls and started making a couple sandwiches. I wasn't sure who they were for until he wrapped them in aluminum foil, put them in a plastic bag, and called me over.

"*¿Te recuerdas dónde trabajan Miguel y Ramón?*" he asked me to see if I remembered how to get back downstairs where the guys were working earlier.

"*¿Abajo?*" I responded for confirmation.

"*Si. ¿Sabes llegar para mandarle estos sándwichitos contigo?*"

I nodded yes, but my dad saw the doubt on my face.

"Okay, *ven para encaminarte*," he said.

He walked me over to aisle 12, which had the double door we had gone through at the opposite end.

"*¿Ves la puerta allá?*"

"*Si,*" I said excitedly, then began walking with purpose.

"*Llevaselo y ven para atras enseguida*," he instructed so I knew to return promptly once my mission was over.

"Okay, *Papi*," I answered over my shoulder.

My heart rate sped up as I pushed through the double door and went down the dingy staircase. I counted the steps as I walked down. Whenever I got nervous or anxious, I used to count things to distract myself from the nerves. Stairs, white sneakers, cracks on the wall, anything that was within eyeshot. When I got to the bottom of the staircase, I looked around and didn't see them at first. Then I heard some boxes being tossed down from a delivery truck outside and slid across the room on this really long waist-high shelf that had metal wheels all over it. Ramón looked over and saw me standing there.

"¿Hey, *Tonito, nos trajiste el lonche?*" Ramón asked, noticing the bag I was carrying.

"*Si, mi papa le mando sándwiches,*" I responded while raising the bag up.

"Oh, good," Ramón said. "That's my favorite lunch. Put it over there, *ensima de esa caja*, please."

"Okay," I obliged.

I knew my dad told me to go right back up, but you know, attention spans. I stood watching, in awe of the fluidity in which the truck driver tossed Miguel boxes, which he slid down to Ramón, who caught them, put them on the long waist-high shelf with metal wheels, and slid them across the room.

Ramón noticed and asked, "You want to try?"

I nodded, and he called me over.

"*La caja viene dura cuando el la tira, okay. Yo la agarro y te la paso a ti.* Then you slide it down that way," he said as he pointed.

"Okay," I responded.

And the first box came down hard and fast, like he said it would. He stopped it with the hand he had a glove on, spun around, and placed it on the shelf for me. "Okay, take it away," he said.

I kept my hands on the box as I ran alongside the rolling shelf and slid it across almost all the way to the end before I let it go and watched it land where all the other boxes were.

"Good job, but you got to be fast. *Ven para atrás*," Ramón said, as he already had two more boxes waiting.

I slid the first one down, which didn't make it all the way to the end, and then the second, which landed right behind it. I was clearly stifling their progress, so it did not surprise me when Ramón said, "Okay, one more, little man." He handed it to me, and I ran alongside with it and finished pushing all three boxes the full way.

"Good job, Tony Junior. *Dile gracias a tu papi*," said Ramón.

"Okay. Bye, Ramón," I said as I ran up the stairs, excited to tell my dad how I helped.

I got up the stairs and ran down the aisle and around the deli counter. My dad was servicing a customer.

"Half a pound of Boar's Head ham," the man requested in a monotone voice.

"Sure, sure," my dad responded as he quickly grabbed a hunk of ham; placed it on the slicer machine that he told me never to get near; put down a sheet of parchment paper, which he had pre-folded a bunch of during his morning preparation; and began slicing. I wanted to wait for him to finish, but I couldn't contain myself.

"Pa, *yo ayude a Ramón y a Miguel*," I blurted out, excited that I'd helped the guys with their work.

"*¿O, si? Wow, que bueno. ¿Qué hiciste?*" he asked, wondering how I helped while he weighed the sliced meat on the scale. Then he looked over at the customer and said, "This is my son."

The customer seemed to be as uninterested as his voice sounded.

"Anything else?" my dad asked with a smile.

"No," the grumpster responded as he grabbed his ham and waddled away.

"*¿Y que hiciste? Dime*," my dad asked me.

"*Me dierón cajas que vinierón en un delivery, y yo la lleve en el slide al otro lado*," I said.

"*¿Oh, ya llego el delivery de Krasdale?*" he interrupted.

"Uh-huh," I said as I nodded in agreement, even though I didn't know where the delivery was from. "*Y yo tire la caja lejo en el shelf largo que tieno wheels.*"

"*Que tiene ruedas*," he corrected.

"*Si*," I responded.

"*Que bueno, mi hijo. Va ser buen trabajador tu.*"

"*Aja*," I agreed, then added, "I want to work here one day, just like you."

"No, *mi hijo*," my dad responded as he shook his head and smiled. "*Tu tienes que ir a la escuela, seguir siendo un estudiante sobresaliente, grauduarte de la universidad y despues vas a tener un trabajo profesional. Con corbata puesta, y en una oficina. Y ahi, tu vas a ser un buen trabajador.*"

I let that marinate for a minute. That was the first time I can remember internalizing that my father's efforts, hard work, and sacrifices had more to do with his goals for me and our family than with his goals for himself.

Carmen walked over sipping a juice. She slid open one of my dad's fridge doors and put it in.

"*Tony, voy dejar el juguito aqui para que no se me caliente*," she said.

"Okay," my dad responded.

"*¿Tonito, quiere hacer chavo?*" she asked me, wanting to know if I would like to make some money.

I gave her a stare that meant "I don't know what you're talking about, but I'm in."

"*Ven ayudarme un ratito, te voy a enseñar a empacar,*" she said. "*Tony, me lo voy a llevar para que me empaque,*" she told my dad.

I looked over to see if it was okay with him or not, as he turned away from servicing another customer.

"*Si, si vallen,*" he said, and I did.

Carmen was cool. She quickly became one of my favorite people at the supermarket. She was a cashier and taught me how to pack bags for the customers. She taught me to double-bag and to place heavier items like cans and jars on the bottom and lighter items on top. Meat should always be individually wrapped in a single bag before putting it into a double bag, to avoid it leaking blood onto other items. Eggs and bread always went in separate single bags no matter what. Even if the customer only bought two things. Even if they only bought bread and eggs, separate them. I liked that she didn't speak to me like I was a kid and even cussed sometimes around me. Whenever an aggravated customer didn't like how I packed or complained, she'd defend me to them and help me fix what I did wrong.

"*Tonito, no puede poner el pan debajo de algo duro. Lo vas a machucar. Todo los que es asi va en una bolsa separrada,*" she would instruct.

"Okay, Carmen," I responded politely.

When a customer didn't tip or was stingy, she'd let them have it.

"*¿No me le va dar nada al niño?* He's working hard too," she'd say.

It was toward the end of my dad's shift already, so I told Carmen I had to go.

"*Okay, Tonito, gracias. Ven ayudame mañana,*" she said.

Her inviting me back made me happy, because I figured I must've not done that bad of a job.

I was about to walk away when she said, "*Esperate, llevate tu chavo, eso es tuyo, papito*," she said as she pointed to my small bucket of change. "*Ven, para cambiartelo. Pero siempre cuenta tu chavo primero.*" Then she helped me to count my earnings as she spread it all out, counted it up, opened the register, and gave me the equivalent in bills.

I didn't really think I was going to get to keep the money. That day, I made about $3.85 in a couple of hours. I ran over to my dad, ecstatic.

"*Papi, mira*," I told him, as I held up the bills and loose change.

"*Wow, te ganaste todo eso?*" he asked.

"*Si!*" I responded.

"*¿Y trabajaste bien?*" he asked, making sure my mind should be on doing good work.

"*Si, y Carmen me dijo que venga mañana a trabajar otravez*," I added.

"*Mañana no, papi*," my dad responded. "*El día es muy largo los sábados. Pero yo te traigo el Lunes.*"

"Okay," I said as the news momentarily burst my bubble, but then I remembered my fistful of cash and started smiling again.

"*¿Que tu va hacer con el dinero tuyo?*" my dad asked to gauge my financial prudence.

"*Le voy dar uno a ti, uno a mami, uno a manito*," I responded, as I was splitting up my earnings in my head without really doing the math.

"*No, papito, a mi no me tienes que dar nada*," my dad responded. "*Mejor guardalo para que quando comienze la escuela, tenga tu dinerito.*"

Saving my money for when school started was way

better advice than what I had planned. Left to my own devices, I would have given away half of my earnings and been hopped-up on M&M's before dinner time.

"Okay, Pa," I said as Norma walked in.

She worked the deli from 2 p.m. to closing time. She was nice and gave me a big hug as if I knew her already. My dad told her about the orders he was going to put in for stuff that was running low and reminded her to write down anything else she thought they may need. With that, we left and were on our way home. Two hardworking dudes after a long day.

That weekend was a blur to me. I couldn't wait until Monday came back around so I could go with my dad again. If it were up to me, I would have gone every single day. When I went back on Monday, I hung out with the guys downstairs around lunch time, packed bags for Carmen again, and, best of all, bonded some more with Dad. It was slower on Monday, so I only made $2.65. Tuesday, I made $4.25, and Wednesday, $3.50.

On Wednesday when I went to take the guys their lunch, there wasn't a delivery coming in that I could help with. They were breaking down boxes and tying them up.

"*Hey, Tonito. ¿Quieres aprender un acertijo?*"

"*¿Que es eso?*" I asked.

"*¿No sabes que es eso?*" responded Miguel. "*Es como una canción o una poema pero mas pequeña.*"

"*Es un riddle,*" added Ramón.

"*Oh okay. Si yo se,*" I responded, acknowledging that I knew what a riddle was.

"Okay, repeat it with me," Miguel said in broken English.

"*Entre melón y melambe,*" he said.

"*Entre melón y…*" I repeated but blanked out on the last word.

"*Melambe*," Ramón chimed in as he continued breaking down boxes with his box cutter and stepping on them.

"*Entre melón y melambe*," I said.

"*Matarón un pajarito*," Miguel continued.

"*Matarón un pajarito*," I repeated.

"*Melón se comio las plumas*," continued Miguel

"*Melón se comio la pluma*," I repeated.

"*Y Melambe es el pajarito*," he finished with a big smile, and Ramón began laughing.

"*¿Y Melambe que?*" I said as I laughed along, even though I didn't get it.

"*Melambe es el pajarito*," Miguel repeated. "*¿Okay, te lo aprendiste para que se lo diga a tu papi?*"

"*Dejame ver*," I said as I recalled the riddle. "*Entre melambe y melón…no, no*," I quickly self-corrected. "*Entre melón y melambe, matarón un pajarito. ¿Ummm, melón?*"

"*Si, melón se comio las plumas y melambe es el pajarito*," Miguel added.

Then I said it from beginning to end three times back-to-back, each time Miguel and Ramón laughing even harder.

"*Okay, Tony Junior, ve dile a tu pai*" said Ramón.

I ran back upstairs to tell my dad the new riddle I learned. "*Papi, papi!*" I shouted with excitement.

"*Dime, mi hijo*," he responded.

"*Aprendi una nuevo riddle.*"

"*¿Si? ¿Quien te lo enseño, Carmen?*" he asked.

"*No, Miguel y Ramón*," I responded.

"*Oh, okay, dime la. ¿Como es?*" he asked, wanting me to recite the riddle.

"*Entre melón y melambe matarón un pajarito. Melón se comio las plumas, Y melambe es el pajarito.*"

I waited for my dad to burst out in laughter like the guys had, but he didn't. He did smile and shake his head, though, and that's about the same thing coming from him. He shook his head in a "they pranked me" sort of way.

"*Estuvo buena esa,*" he told me, and although I still didn't fully get the riddle, he made me feel like I was part of their inside joke.

The next day, I had a doctor's appointment that my mom took me to, so I couldn't go to work with my dad. I was eager to get back on Friday, especially since I knew I would not get to go all weekend. It was a good day for me. I made $8.00! My biggest take to date. The supermarket was buzzing, and Carmen was telling me how much busier it gets on Saturdays.

"*¿Vas a venir mañana?*" she asked, to find out if I was coming or not.

"*No,*" I said sadly. "*Mañana Papi trabaja tarde y dijo que yo me cansaría.*"

"*Oh okay. ¿Y tu crees que te cansaría?*" she asked.

"*No, yo puedo trabajar mucho también. Todos los días,*" I responded.

"*Pues ve dile a tu papi, que Carmen necesitas tu ayuda mañana, y que quieres que tú venga,*" she suggested.

"*¿De verdad?*" I asked to make sure she wasn't messing with me.

"*Si, ve dile,*" she replied, "*Vamos a ver lo que el dice. Si dice que no, no perdemos nada con preguntar. Ya tienes el 'no,' tengamos que buscar el 'si.'*"

I made my way toward the deli, heart racing. I rarely asked my dad for stuff, not directly anyway. I'd usually try my mom as a litmus test first. These were extreme times, though. If I waited until I'd get home, he and my mom would both say no for sure. Here, I could speak to him man-to-man. Coworker-to-coworker. He'd be proud that I'm willing and wanting to work so hard. Plus, Carmen having my back was like having an ace up my sleeve. I didn't think I could lose.

"*Pa*," I said in a tone that hinted at me wanting something.

"*Dime, papi*," he responded.

"*¿Yo puedo venir mañana?*" I asked, wanting to come to work with him regardless of Saturday being his double-shift day.

"*Tu sabes que mañana es sábado, papi*," he replied. "*El día es muy largo. Y tú no puedes dejar a mami sola el día entero*."

"*Es nadamas un día*," I said, "*y Carmen dijo que necesita mi ayuda*."

"*¿O si?*" my dad responded. "*¿Y no vas a llorar o cansarte mucho?*" he asked, worried that I'd cry or get too tired if I came.

"*No!*" I said excitedly at the thought of him considering it.

"*Bueno*," he responded. "*Vamos a ver lo que diga mami cuando lleguemos hoy*."

After we got home, my mom proved to be a harder sell. I nagged her all afternoon, offered to do chores, and said I'd go to bed super early. My dad eventually cosigned, probably because he was tired of hearing me whine about it, and she finally gave in. I was so ecstatic that I washed the dishes after we ate, showered, and picked out my clothes for the next day. I also skipped playing Sega Genesis with my brother and went to bed early, just like I said I would. I wasn't tired and was super excited, so I didn't fall asleep right away even though I wanted to so that I could pull tomorrow into today that much sooner.

When dawn became dusk and our day began, we were off to the races. It was a hard workday for anyone, I'm sure, and I was pulling it off at seven years old. I was packing like a pro. I had a stack of double bags set up for my own little version of morning preparation, and I added to that stockpile whenever there was a fleeting lull between customers. If Carmen went on break or didn't have a customer, I hopped over to her neighbor Gloria's line and bagged for her. I was in a grocery-bagging flow state. It was my fight night. My game day. And I crushed it. I was hopped-up on the sugar and caffeine I had from two cans of soda. I spent $1.50 of my own money in the vending machine, on a Sunkist and a Welch's grape, which were exotic compared to the Coke and Pepsi I was used to at home. I also spent $0.25 on a gumball and $0.50 on one of those sticky, stretchy hand toys that came in those see-through plastic bubbles with a red bottom. Even after all that spending, I raked in $17.88! I was ecstatic. Exhausted and carrying a brand new appreciation for my dad's ability to wake up early and put in the work for his family day in and day out, but ecstatic nonetheless.

The summer was coming to a close with the new school year just a couple of weeks out. That epic Saturday wound up being the second to last day I went to work with my dad that summer, and one of the most memorable for sure.

During the last week before school started, my dad gave my mom some money for the school supplies my brother and I needed. My list was longer and contained things like three black-and-white marble notebooks, two No. 2 pencils, one red pen, which excited me because I'd never used one before. I always thought they were strictly for teachers.

We were walking down the aisles of one of the stores on Liberty Ave when I saw it. The pencil case of all pencil cases. The Red Rider BB gun of pencil cases. It was a rectangular box like most but had a plastic trapper-keeper like padding on it and a rad design. It was blue and had these light gray drawers lining the base, which—wait for it—sprung open with the touch of a button! How dope is that?? There was even a button on the side that made a six-inch ruler pop out. I could use one drawer for my eraser, another for a sharpener, one for paper clips, and I was sure I'd find use for the others. I turned it over to look at the price tag, and it was $15.99. There was no way my mom would be able to get it for me. That was almost half of my entire school supply budget. I put it down and walked away dejected, but then I had a mini epiphany. I had $17 of my hard-earned dollars in my pocket!

I continued to walk around the store with my mom while I mustered up the gumption to shoot my shot and ask her if I could buy it.

"*¿Cuanto cuesta?*" she asked.

"*Fifteen dollars,*" I responded, leaving out the $0.99, plus tax.

"*¿Tu esta loco, muchacho? Eso es demasiado caro para eso. Compra unos de esos,*" she said as she pointed to a bulky rectangular plastic pencil case that was as devoid of style as it was empty inside. But it only cost $3.99.

"*Ma,*" I responded, announcing my last-ditch effort. "*Pero yo tengo mi dinero tambien,*" I reassured.

"*Bueno,*" she responded. "*Tu debería guardar ese dinero.*" She suggested I should save my money.

"*¿Para que?*" I asked. I just learned about earning, and as the money burned a hole in my pocket, saving was an alien concept to me.

"*Siempre se debería guardar algo, mi hijo. Uno nunca sabe lo de mañana,*" she said. "*Pero, tu trabajaste por ese dinero, y puedes comprar lo que quieras,*" she added.

My eyes opened up as wide as my smile expanded ear-to-ear. Her words of wisdom about saving for a rainy day wafted past my little ears and all I heard was the part about being able to do what I chose with the money I earned. I thanked her, then ran over and grabbed my pencil case. The most exhilarating thing was that it was the last one left!

At the register, I reached into my pocket, pulled out my black and red Velcro wallet, and handed over my slightly crumbled and folded $17.00 to my mom.

She took $10.00 and handed me back $7.00. "*Toma, mi hijo, guarda eso para que pueda comprar algo en la escuela,*" she said.

My mom figured she would have spent $4.00–$5.00 on a pencil case anyway, so she subsidized the one I wanted so that I didn't blow all of my money on one purchase. She was resourceful like that.

That pencil case was my pride and joy. On day one of school, I placed it at the top of my desk, perfectly parallel with the edge, while some classmates, I was sure, gazed over in astonishment. To me, a glow was radiating off of it. It was the most amazing thing I owned. It was the most fulfilling purchase I've made to date. The culmination of hard work yielding results that cultivated my desires.

As the excitement of starting a new school year inevitably faded, the mundanity that came along with a long year of lessons and endless homework assignments took hold. What became of that pencil case as the year churned on is as good a guess of yours as it is of mine. I'd like to say that I still have it, that it occupies a spot on some prized-possession mantle, but I vaguely recall it eventually beginning to deteriorate as the things of children do. Springs became sprung, some of the gray plastic draws wouldn't open, others wouldn't close. I'm sure I ruined the exterior with stickers that I had second thoughts about and removed while leaving behind that sticky cotton-like residue. Where the physical pieces of it wound up, however, wasn't as important as its lasting impact. It was the first major purchase I made with money I earned, and it watered the seed that my father planted via his exemplary work ethic. It reinforced the importance of responsibility and highlighted the fact that hard work really did pay off.

NOSTRAND AVE

Henry woke up and went through his morning routines as quietly as possible so that he wouldn't wake Dolores. But no luck. As usual, she barely got any sleep the night before. Too busy worrying. He'd graduated from the police academy barely six months ago and had a late night to early morning shift.

"Did you put on your vest?" she asked.

"I did, babe. Don't worry," he replied.

"You know I can't stop worrying until after you're home, and still...hours later, you're gone again," said Dolores.

"Come here, babe," he told her as he sat down at the side of the bed. "I won't be on this shift too much longer. Once I hit the one-year mark, I'll be able to put in for a transfer."

"The next six months can't pass soon enough," she replied. "Be safe out there. And call me every chance you get."

"Will do, babe. I love you. Try to get some sleep."

Out he went to his post, where he met up with his partner. "Martineeez," he greeted the fellow officer.

"What's going on, brother?" Martinez responded.

"Not much," said Henry. "Here, got you a coffee."

"Who's better than you? Thanks, man," said Martinez. "The lieutenant wants us covering the A train and walking the perimeter of some of the red-zone stations."

"Okay, cool. Lead the way," replied Henry.

"You'll like it. Ride some trains, look at the pretty ladies going to work, bullshit on the platforms. Easy money," said Martinez.

On the other side of town, Tracy was being woken up for school by her loving mother. "Wake up, you fat, lazy bitch," yelled Ms. Walker.

"Mom! What the fuck? I'm up. Damn. Why you always gotta be so damn loud?" Tracy replied.

"This my house. I'll be as loud as I want," she said. "You ain't gonna wind up like me," she continued while taking a sip of her morning cocktail of Gin and Sunny Delight. Tracy's father had been an abusive alcoholic who left three days shy of her second birthday, dumping them without notice and already behind on the bills. He'd driven Tiffany Walker to drink, the only remnant he left behind.

"I hope not," Tracy said with an attitude.

"Don't make me slap the shit outta you. Get your fat ass up and go to school."

As she was leaving the house for her hour and a half commute, Tracy asked her mom for some money for the train.

"Where the fuck is your school MetroCard?"

"I lost it," Tracy replied.

"Well, that sounds like a personal issue," said Ms. Walker.

"How am I supposed to get to school?" Tracy asked.

"Figure it out. And what you *need* to do is stop eating them damn candy bars and get you an apple. That's why you look like that," commented Ms. Walker.

"Whatever," Tracy said as she walked out and slammed the door.

She walked over to the Nostrand Avenue A train, went downstairs, and pretended to buy a MetroCard at the machine while waiting for both the attendant to become distracted and her train to approach the platform so she could try to hop the turnstiles.

While taking a fifteen-minute break, Officer Henry stood a bit off to the side texting his wife, "Everything has gone smooth today, babe, and my shift will be over soon. Love you."

An announcement came over the loudspeaker. "There will be a downtown-bound A train approaching the station in approximately two minutes."

Tracy looked around to assess the situation while more passengers swiped through the turnstiles. The rumblings of the approaching train rose to a crescendo and her heart rate elevated in unison. She was not the most athletic girl and hadn't really tried anything like this since she was a kid when her mom used to make her duck down underneath the turnstiles. She fumbled it at first, not getting her leg up high enough and dropping back to the ground on the side she was trying to leave. The attendant saw and sounded the alarm before she finally hoisted herself up and over.

Henry quickly ran over to meet her on the other side.

"Officer! Officer!" the attendant yelled as he stepped out of the booth to point Tracy out. "It was her. Arrest her!"

"I ain't do nothing," said Tracy.

"Excuse me, ma'am, do you have some ID?" Henry

asked, remembering his training dictated that he should always identify first.

"No, I ain't got no license. I'm sixteen, and I'm in school," Tracy replied.

The train arrived and people began boarding.

"I'm going to have to ask you to come with me and sit over here then, ma'am. We're holding up traffic," said Henry.

Sizing up the officer who was about her height and much thinner, Tracy said, "I told you I ain't do nothin', and I need to go to school. That man crazy."

At this point, the train left and there were fewer people around.

"Arrest her, Officer. Giver her a ticket!" shouted the attendant.

"Fuck you, asshole," Tracy shouted back at him.

"You mother bitch, you," says the man.

Since this was his first time dealing with something like this alone, Henry called in this escalating situation on his radio to alert his partner. Then he told the attendant, "Sir, I'm going to have to ask you to please go back into your booth and let me do my job."

The attendant was visibly upset, but he obliged.

"You gonna make me miss my next train too, Officer? Shoot! I got a quiz in first period."

"Ma'am, I want to get you on your way as soon as possible, but I need you to work with me. You're getting a citation for jumping the train," Henry said, pulling out his summons booklet. "So I need you to cooperate and give me your full name, date of birth, and address."

"What's that? A ticket?" Tracy asked.

"It's a summons. You will receive a court date in the

mail, to which a parent or legal guardian will have to accompany you and pay a fine," replied Henry.

"Oh my God, are you serious?!" she said, her voice cracking as the tears welled up in the corner of her eyes. "That man is lying. Why you only believe him? All I want to do is go to school. You know what my momma will do to me if I get in trouble here?"

"Ma'am, this will go a lot faster if you cooperate," Henry replied.

An announcement came over the loudspeaker. "There will be a downtown-bound express A train approaching the station in approximately four minutes."

Henry pointed upward with one finger and asked, "You hear that? Do you want to make that train, or do you want to miss your quiz and have your mom upset about that too?"

"Man, I ain't even gonna take the damn train then," Tracy said as she took a step toward the exit.

"Ma'am, you're not free to go," said Henry as he reached for her right wrist.

"Get off me! Get your hands *off* me," she yelled, calling even more attention to the situation.

Henry stepped in front of her, and she slapped the summons booklet from his left hand and tried to run for the emergency exit door next to the turnstiles, but the attendant disabled it. Henry grabbed her by the arm and reached for his cuffs.

Screaming and crying hysterically, she kept pulling her hands away as he tried to restrain her up against that exit door. "I can't get in trouble! I didn't do nothing. Leave me alone. Stop it! Stop it!" Tracy pleaded, knocking his handcuffs to the ground.

Protocol now allowed Henry to use force. He reached for

his club, and she flailed her arms frantically. She accidentally hit his firearm, releasing the safety clip on his holster. Henry hit her on the leg with his club to get her to the ground.

Several people on the platform had begun recording this on their phones. "Leave her alone," one person shouted. "She didn't do anything. This is abuse," another chimed in. "You can't hit her. Get his badge number. This is brutality," added a third.

Henry's reactions to everything grew increasingly nervous, and Tracy's crying and shouting weren't helping. He hit her with the club again, and she dropped to the ground, followed by the crowd becoming rowdier. He grabbed the cuffs and got one on her right wrist.

The attendant was on the phone with 911, reporting the incident, and more units were on the way. Still kicking and screaming wildly, Tracy wound up scratching Henry across the face. Martinez ran over as Tracy hit Henry in the nose and then Henry drew his weapon. His nervous hand slipped, and he dropped the gun. Henry and Tracy tried to grab the firearm simultaneously. In the tussle for control of the weapon, one of their fingers found the trigger and the gun went off. Martinez, close enough now to witness this, drew his firearm as well. Then he saw his partner was clinching his waist-side and falling backward. Tracy was screaming and still holding onto Henry's gun. Without hesitation, Martinez unloaded five shots at her torso...fatally wounding the high schooler.

Within twenty-four hours, Dolores sat weeping at Henry's bedside in a post-op hospital room, while half a dozen of his brothers in blue, including Martinez, paced the waiting area, waiting for Henry to wake up. They'd sent two uniformed officers over to Tracy's home to inform her family of what had happened.

Ms. Walker all but attacked the officers as she broke down crying. "You killed my baby! You killed my little girl! Nooooo, noooo. You sons of bitches, when are you going to leave us alone, you evil devils?" she declared.

"Ma'am, we're deeply sorry for your loss," said one of the officers when he was finally able to get a word in edgeways.

"She was a good girl. Jesus why?!" she continued.

"Mrs. Walker—"

"It's Miss, you no good piece of shit," she replied.

"Here's the address to the hospital where you need to claim your daughter. We can take you if you'd like," the officer said.

"I don't want nothing from you. I can take myself," she spat at them.

"Okay, well, here's our card. Contact us when you're sobered up if you'd like to make a statement," he said.

"Fuck you! I ain't drunk. Get out of my home. Get out!" Ms. Walker responded.

SEVERAL MONTHS LATER, a woman walked into her neighborhood police precinct in her Sunday church dress, right after that morning's service. She engaged an irritated police officer working the front desk who seemed angry at life, and she could smell alcohol on his breath as he spoke.

"Yes, ma'am, how can I help you," Officer Kurth asked the woman.

"Hello, sir. My name is Tiffany Walker, and I wanted to

get a list of all the after-school community centers in the area," she requested.

It had been several months, and although he still had nightmares of the incident, he didn't make the connection as to who this woman was right away.

"All the community centers in our jurisdiction get posted on that bulletin board over there," he replied, pointing at a corkboard by the entrance.

"Oh okay, thank you," responded Ms. Walker. "Do you have a sheet of paper and a pen I can borrow to jot down the names and phone numbers?"

"Hold on," he responded grumpily. Henry rolled his wheelchair out from under his desk and over to the supply drawer to grab a legal pad and pen. "Here you go," he said as he handed them over to her.

"Thank you kindly, Officer...Henry Kurth, is it?" Ms. Walker asked.

"That's right," Henry said as she walked over to the bulletin board.

He looked at the nameplate on his desk, wondering how she knew his first name because the name tag on his uniform only showed his last name. The nameplate on his desk read P.O. Kurth. He looked up at her while she jotted down some of the information, realizing she looked familiar. He made the connection, remembering her name from the loads of paperwork for the Tracy Walker case.

Immediately he became suspicious. *Why is she here?* He felt there had to be an ulterior motive.

She walked back over to his desk and handed him the legal pad and pen after ripping out the two sheets she'd used. Smiling, she said, "Thank you, Officer Kurth. I'm going to give this information to my pastor, see if we can get these kids engaged in some positive activities after school, so that we can avoid the inexcusable police harassment that has been going on lately."

"We do our best to service the productive members of our community such as yourself, Ms. Walker," Henry replied.

As she was about to turn away and leave, Tiffany said, "I almost forgot, I've got something for you." She reached into her purse.

Henry tensed up for half a second.

"I reckon you'll be needing this more than I ever did." She pulled out a stainless-steel liquor flask and placed it right in front of him on his desk.

He stared at it and said nothing.

She stopped smiling and left.

BULLY

Q ueens, New York circa 1994

"TODAY IS A VERY IMPORTANT DAY," said Mr. K. "As you all know, we voted last Thursday to make this year's fourth-grade class play *Cinderella* and today we find out who our Cinderella and Prince Charming will be!"

A nervous murmur sprinkled with excitement made its way around the classroom among the kids.

Mr. K continued, "Let me explain the selection process to you. Anyone can volunteer for these two roles. I will put a passage from the play up on the chalkboard. One by one, all the volunteers will come up to the front of the class and read the passage to us the same way you would on stage. The rest of us will make mental notes on how well you do, so that we can all vote to select the best person for the role later. After all the volunteers have showcased their acting chops, I'm going to ask them to step outside, into the hallway, while the rest of us quietly vote. The person with the most votes will win the starring role. And when you become big movie stars in Hollywood, don't forget who discovered you." He laughed with that deep, breath-pausing laugh of his.

I sat nervously at my hard wooden desk in the middle-right side of the room, looking around at all the shy, awkward, soon-to-volunteer faces and all the seemingly more confident "there's-no-way-in-Hell-I'm-going-up-there" faces in the room.

"Speak amongst yourselves and decide if you will audition for the rest of us today while I write the passages for both Cinderella and our prince on the chalkboard. Remember that all of us will play a part in the play on or off stage."

Should I audition for the starring role? I thought. *It is the first step to being discovered and on my way to Hollywood. Then I can be in a movie...or maybe even the Power Rangers! Or should I be the stagehand guy who opens and closes the curtains with those long, thick ropes that look like the ones we climb in gym class? That could be fun too, I guess.*

"Hey, Anthony," the most angelic voice in the whole wide world whispered. "Are you going to audition to be the prince?"

"I will if you audition for Cinderella," I told Stephanie, mentally giving myself a pat on the back for such a smooth comeback.

"Yea right," she says. "I'm too much of a scaredy-cat for that. I wouldn't be able to speak in front of the whole fourth, fifth, and sixth grades!"

Oh, man, I hadn't even thought of that. I was worried about speaking just in front of our class...imagine the actual play in front of the whole school in six weeks?

"Take two more minutes to make your decisions, kids,"

said Mr. K. "Who is the board monitor for this week, by the way?"

"I am, Mr. K," said Sue-Ellen.

"Please make sure you clap the erasers outside the window today. They're filthy."

"Yes, Mr. K," she replied with an eye roll.

Why she signed up to be board monitor beat me. She hated it and was always complaining about the dusty chalk making her cough. I enjoyed being board monitor and trying to make gigantic clouds of chalk when I clapped the erasers together. Two weeks ago, I clapped them so fast that even Leo was impressed and didn't take my cookies at lunch that day.

"Okay, my lovely Cinderellas, ladies first. Stand up at your desks if you'd like to audition."

All of us eagerly scanned the room, waiting for the brave souls to stand up. One by one, both of the twins, Vickyana and Iliana, stood, then Tiffany, Angela, Pamela, and Renee got up too. Six girls in all.

"Okay, Cinderellas, go stand in the back of the room, and I'll call you up one by one to the front. Read the paragraph for us and then return to your seats. Angela, we'll start with you."

She walked up to the front of the classroom, nervously giggling. Everyone liked Angela. She was sweet. She was also Steph's best friend, so that meant she'd be like my sister-in-law or something one day.

Angela twirled her braided hair around as she read the paragraph on the board and giggled. The class would laugh with her every time. She finished, we all clapped and smiled, and with a huge look of relief on her face, she went back to her desk and started talking with Steph right in front of me.

"You're so cool, Angie," Stephanie told her. "I wish I could do that."

"Thanks," replied Angela as she turned around to me and said, "Ant, go up there. You'll do great."

I nervously nodded my head and smiled, completely tuning out Tiffany's read.

"Thank you, Tiffany," said Mr. K. "You can go back to your seat now. It's your turn, Pamela."

Pam was cute and had really nice blonde hair, and last year in third grade, she was Ariel from *The Little Mermaid* in Ms. Soto's class. She was outstanding and knew what she was doing. But my heart belonged to Stephanie and always would. Right then, it dawned on me. The plan of all plans. If I got the part, Steph would have to love me back. Who doesn't love a prince? That was my motivation. I had to win her over somehow. Even if I didn't get it, she'd think I was just as cool as Angela, and that was one step closer to making her my girlfriend.

The roaring clap in the room snapped me out of my plotting mind.

"Great job, Pamela," said Mr. K. "Very impressive. Please take your seat now."

After the remaining girls went up, Mr. K asked them all to step out into the hallway. Then he whispered to us, "Okay, my little Siskel and Eberts, by a show of hands, how many of you want Angela to be our Cinderella?" He counted the votes and tallied them up next to where he had written all the volunteers' names.

We all knew Pamela was going to win, but my loyalty vote, together with Steph's, went to Angie.

"Ralphy, please let the girls know they can come in now," said Mr. K.

Ralphy's seat was right by the door, so he reached over

and opened the door. "Mr. K said to come back in," he told the girls.

As they walked in, Mr. K said, "Everyone give a round of applause to our Cinderella, Pamela."

She smiled wide, sort of bouncing with each step she was so excited.

Good for her, I thought. She definitely deserved it.

"Okay, everyone back to their seats. Quiet down. Now, time for our leading man. Which of you brave young men will audition for the role?"

My heart was racing like a marching-band snare drum solo. Leo got up, then Ralphy, Mike, Joey, Curtis, and even Charlie got up, and then Steven did too. Steph turned around to me and gave me a pouty, sad face, so I darted up like a Whac-A-Mole in a town fair.

"Okay, guys, to the back of the room you go. Curtis, we'll start with you."

Curtis went up and could've given an Oscar-worthy performance for all I knew. Drowning waves of nervousness overwhelmed my consciousness. What was I thinking? Last year I had a one-liner in the class play as Peddler 2 in a *Pinocchio* parody and nearly shit myself. Now I'm auditioning for a starring role in my second performance ever? Talk about being overzealous. *She better love me after doing this,* I swore. And not some love-me-today, knew-me-tomorrow kind of love. I meant *love*-love. Love me like Topanga loved Corey or how Kelly loved Zack before Jeff came along, kind of love.

"Okay, who wants to go next?" Mr. K asked as Leo nudged me forward in the line.

"A brave volunteer," says Mr. K. "Come on up, Anthony."

I turn and look over my shoulder at Leo with a glare

that must have been a fusion of disdain and a deer caught in the headlights. "Stupid jerk," I murmured as I walked toward the green chalkboard.

He smirked at me with that maniacal, devilish smile of his that only accentuated his horn-like eyebrows.

I looked at Steph as I walked by her desk, and she pointed at something she'd written on her desk. It was a heart with our initials in it! A+S, it said. And it wasn't written in pencil—it was in pen! She'd have to spit on it to wipe it off. Suddenly I had the confidence to take a role away from Macaulay Culkin.

"Read the paragraph off the board and project your voice toward the audience as if you were on stage. Ready? Action!" said Mr. K.

I cleared my throat and gave it a whirl.

"How foolish of me to expect to find my true love in just one night by throwing a grand ball for all the fairest eligible ladies of the town to attend. What was I thinking? I've been somber and alone for far too long, causing me to resort to these drastic measures."

I didn't realize the next portion was stage direction and almost whispered, "Enter Cinderella as the ballroom doors open up wide," getting a few chuckles from the class.

"Wait! There is my princess. True love has finally answered my prayers. She is as beautiful as an April morning. Come, let us dance." Finished, I started back toward my seat with my head held high and a little extra pep in my step.

That was my debut of some pretty impressive acting chops, if I do say so myself. The class clapped and everything. They may have clapped for everyone else, but I was too nervous to remember. I even caught Leo turning to Joey and saying something to the effect of "that was good," as I walked back to my seat. Angie turned to me and said, "You're so gonna win," and Steph nodded in agreement as she blushed.

Knowing I was awesome, I smiled back at them and said, "Nahhh. We'll see what happens."

Leo tried pushing Joey up next like he did to me, so that he would go last, but Mr. K actually noticed this time.

"Leo, since you're so kind to let people go before you, how about we return the favor and let you go first? Come up," he said sternly.

Then Leo walked by and kicked my chair on his way up to the front of the room, hard enough to make me lose my balance but soft enough to act like it was an accident. What an evil douche.

Leo read his lines with a lackluster I'm-too-cool-for-school attitude, looking at the floor the whole time, sucking his teeth, and messing up and repeating his lines. Then as he went to his desk he said, "That was stupid. I didn't feel like doing it good."

Joey went up after and gave a similarly forgetful performance, then off we went to stand outside in the hall as the class voted.

We were all slightly on edge while waiting for the results. Leo turned to address us all and surprisingly said, "Guys, no matter what, none of us can get mad. We're all friends, and it doesn't matter who won."

Shocked by his maturity, we all nodded our heads and agreed.

"Yea," said Mike, "we all gave it our best shots."

This was great. I knew I did great, like that feeling you have when you ace an exam before you actually receive the results. I thought Mike did really well, and he was Pamela's boyfriend so he might get a lot of votes just based on that.

He was cool too, so I was okay with that. But I knew for a fact that I smoked Leo and Joey. Curtis I had been too nervous to pay attention to, and the other guys had done so-so. Me and Mike must have been the top choices. So Leo, the class bully, being okay with all that was perfect.

The door opened up with Mr. K at the other side of it, saying, "Come in, my little princes."

All of our names and votes were on the chalkboard, and I had to do a double take as the class clapped to welcome us back in:

Curtis 2

Steven 3

Charlie 1

Mike 5

Ralphy 1

Anthony 12

Leo 2

Joey 1

It was a landslide! Woah, I really won.

"Give it up for our Prince Charming everybody," said Mr. K as he had us take our seats again.

That's so cool. Scary. But good-scary, I thought.

We all took our seats as Mr. K began going over how many practices we were going to have in the classroom and on which days we would get the auditorium to actually practice on the big stage.

"See, I told you so," Angie said.

Steph followed that with, "I knew you would do it for me."

I winked at her and then looked around the room. Steven gave me a nod and a smile. Mike gave me the thumbs up. Pamela smiled and looked eager to go over our lines. I then made it around to Joey and Leo. Joey looked disinterested as usual, sloppily folding up a piece of loose-leaf into a paper airplane. Leo was looking at me like a rabid pit bull who'd had his meal taken away from it. Nostrils flaring, horned eyebrows pointing upward like two little pyramids. Snarling, and pounding his right fist into the palm of his left hand like a Major League Baseball catcher expecting the last pitch of a no-hitter.

I turned around, straight in my desk, acting as if I hadn't seen what I had just seen. Like an ostrich sticking its head in the sand, I found solace in sitting as still as if I was avoiding detection by a Tyrannosaurus rex while in plain sight.

I was partly surprised at the hypocrisy of this kid, and the other part of me felt as if I had been completely in the know all along. While sitting there and perfecting my statue pose, I spent the next two class subjects before lunch talking myself into the possibility that he was joking around, and I had just turned around a half second before he started smiling and did the I'm-just-messin'-with-ya gesture. Then I saw the first one fly past the side of my head in a forward trajectory, soaring between the two girls, headed toward the windows and over the table of plants we'd planted in Styrofoam cups last Wednesday. Pam and Steph both turn around and faced me at the exact same time that I was thinking *What the fuck was that* and began turning my head back.

Wham! Spitball number two hit me and stuck to my cheek, right by my mouth. Everyone who witnessed this, including the girls, burst out into a laugh as I squirmed in a shocked and disgusted, frantic way to slap it off my face.

"Yuck! That almost went in my mouth, stupid," I told Leo. I didn't even know if anyone heard that over all the laughter.

"Hey, hey, settle down back there. This isn't recess. Who wants detention? Who wants detention?!?" When Mr. K actually raises his voice like that, we all listen. Even Leo's bully ass. Right before lunch, about eight minutes before to be exact, I strategically raised my hand and asked, "Can I go to the bathroom? My stomach really hurts."

"Can you hold it?" he replied.

"Nooo," I said. "I really can't."

"Okay, but if we're not here when you return, meet us in the cafeteria. It's almost lunchtime," he said.

I nodded in agreement, having neither the energy nor will to utter an unnecessary word. I felt weak in the knees as I walked out of the room.

I waited until lunch was more than half over, then walked to the cafeteria. Mr. K asked me where I'd been and said that I could still go grab lunch. But I told him my stomach was hurting too much, and I wasn't hungry. I sat there with my head halfway down, on the opposite side of the table from Leo and closer to Mr. K. Maybe he had forgotten that he wanted to kill me, I hoped. Then Mr. K walked away to go speak with Ms. Maloney, a fifth-grade teacher. From the corner of my right eye, I saw Leo get up and start toward me.

"What's wrong with you?" he asked.

"I'm sick," I replied. "I think I have the flu." *Could it be that he was joking all along and I'd just been overreacting? Does he genuinely care about my well-being?* I thought.

I turned my head toward him and noticed him looking toward Mr. K, who was still in deep conversation while Ms. Maloney flirted with him.

"I'm still going to fuck you up," he said as he bounced my forehead off the cold white surface of the fold-a-way lunch table.

I shoved his arm away in a pathetic attempt to fight back as he walked away laughing.

Mr. K walked back to escort us outside for the fifteen minutes of after-lunch recess they give us to burn off some of the sugar we'd ingested at lunch and tire us out enough to be tolerable for the next three hours of class.

"Hey, Ant, you want to play kickball with us outside?" Adam asked me.

"Nah, I don't want to go outside," I replied.

"Come on, you love kickball, and you're one of the best at it. Don't worry about Leo. He's not playing. I think he's playing Asses Up on the handball court with Joey and the fifth graders or something," rebutted Adam.

Is everyone already aware of my impending doom? I thought. I replied, "No, you guys go ahead. I'm going to stay in."

Adam shrugged his shoulders and left with the burgundy kickball under his right arm and a half-squeezed apple juice box in his left hand.

Some of the nerd kids always stayed inside at recess to play checkers and Battleship, and some to start their homework! *Ugh, is this what is going to happen to me? Is this my future?*

The next three torturous hours of sitting in class were a blur. The bell was about to ring for dismissal in like five minutes, and I was out of excuses, plans, or ideas. I looked at Leo with one last piece of hope that he would admit to having just been messing with me all afternoon...and he gave me the finger. Yea, *that* finger.

"Let's start lining up now, in size order, guys and gals," said Mr. K, "so that we can walk out double-file as soon as the first bell rings."

Great, he's speeding up the inevitable, I thought.

The multi-tonal bell rang.

"Okay, let's go, kids. Walk out to the front of staircase B and wait for me to shut off all the lights," said Mr. K.

I stood there with a look on my face that must've been oozing worry. Then it dawned on me. My older brother was picking me up, as he always did after he got out from high school. I was saved! He was a ninth grader, so could put an end to this, or at least scare Leo away. He was usually outside by the time I walked out to the street too. There was a class in front of us, so we were lined up in the staircase, waiting for the second bell, followed by the announcement from the dean, Mr. Laparo, to open the doors.

Above me in the staircase, Leo leaned over Mike's shoulder and said, "I'm gonna fuck you up."

"No, you're not. My brother is outside," I retorted confidently.

"I'll fuck his fat ass up too," Leo replied.

"No, you can't, stupid asshole. Shut up. He's bigger than you," I replied defiantly.

"Shhhh! Keep it down and face forward," said Mr. K.

Can he really beat me and my brother both up? I thought as the worry sank in again.

Right across from me in the girls' line, Stephanie turned to me and asked, "Are you really going to fight Leo?"

I quickly gave a knee-jerk reaction reply. "Hell no," fell from my lips as an of-course-not look spread over my face. I actually thought she would respect me taking the admirable high-road and not succumbing to Leo's bullying taunts and tactics.

The love of my life and future mother of my children leaned over to me and, with an angelic whisper, said, "You're a pussy," then turned away from me in disgust.

At that moment, I felt as if the entire world came

crashing down around me. Everything became dark. I felt as if my heart had leaped up into my throat and was making its way out of my body through my mouth because it didn't even want to be affiliated with me any longer. At that moment, Leo kicking my ass didn't seem like such a bad idea anymore. Maybe he'd knock me unconscious and I'd get amnesia and forget any of this ever happened.

"Okay, kids, see you tomorrow," Mr. K said as he pushed open the brown metal doors after Mr. Laparo's announcement to dismiss us. "Get home safe."

I walked out and scanned the sea of parents, babysitters, and older siblings waiting to make their pickups, searching for my brother who was nowhere to be seen.

Where the fuck is he?! Seriously, today out of all days, he's not here on time?

I get yanked by the top loop of my plastic blue and red Power Rangers backpack and dropped to the floor like a leaf in the fall. It was Leo! I glanced around, realizing a few people had noticed but seemed to think we were horsing around and didn't make much of it. Mike and Adam and even Joey came up behind Leo and held him back as I stood up and he charged forward with the strength of a raging bull. They could barely hold him back!

"Run, go!" Adam said.

"Just get out of here," said Mike.

"Let me go! I'm going to kill him!" Leo exclaimed.

I turned around and ran toward the rear of the school, where the backyard was, frantically dodging people in my way while simultaneously looking for my brother. I got to the backyard and looked back to see the guys still struggling to hold him back and waving me off at the same time. They were yelling, but I couldn't make out what they were saying. I darted across the yard to the other side of the school. I'd never run so fast. The doors on the other side were still open, so I re-entered the school through there. I was safe, for the moment. But now, with no way of getting in touch with my brother, I was essentially trapped inside.

After the longest ten minutes of my life, I walked to the other side of the school looking over my shoulder with every step. I cracked open the brown metal door to the pickup area and stuck my head out. There was barely a handful of people left. Just a couple parent friends catching up before going their separate ways. In the distance, I saw my brother making his way up to my school. I stepped out, looking around one more time to make sure the coast was clear, and then ran toward him with tears in my eyes, but relieved.

"What the hell is wrong with you?" he asked.

"Leo wants to beat me up," I shamefully replied.

"What? Why? Where is he?" he asked.

"I don't know. Let's go home," I said insistently.

"No," he said sternly. "Let's go find him. I think I saw his brother Alvin in school today. He probably came to pick him up. I'll go talk to him."

Like a dog with his tail between his legs, I walked half a step behind my brother.

"There they go over there, standing by the crossing guard," my brother said as he spotted them half a block away.

As we approached them, I felt as if we were about to negotiate some type of gang-war truce over turf or something.

"Yo, what's up?" my brother said to Leo's brother. "Something happened with these two, and he tells me Leo wants to fight him. I want to squash that and make sure we're cool here."

Alvin turned to Leo and said, "That true? Why you wanna fight this kid?"

Leo, half looking up and half looking at the floor while lightly kicking at a few pebbles on the ground, said, "He took my part in the play."

"Nah-uh," I replied quickly. "I won the part fair and square."

Alvin smirked and told Leo, "C'mon, man, you can't be bullying kids, acting like a tough guy. You do that shit when you get to junior high, not now. Don't be doing stuff like that."

How screwed up is this family? I thought. *Put off your bullying until you're older? Like it's some sort of rite of passage. What kind of advice is that? Mental note to self, don't go to the same junior high as this lunatic.*

"So, are we good here?" my brother asked them with a no-nonsense tone in his voice.

"Yea, we're good," Alvin replied, giving my brother a pound. "Shake his hand and say sorry," he instructed Leo as he pointed to me.

And he did. He slapped me five and said, "See you tomorrow," and they walked away. It was finally over. My brother had successfully negotiated my freedom.

"You're the best!" I told him. "Thank you!" I happily walked beside him on our way home.

"When we get home, clean my white sneakers with the soap and toothbrush," he told me.

"Okay, no problem," I said with a smile. Small price to pay for saving my life.

"And clean up our room by yourself for the next month too. If you don't, I'll tell Leo to beat you up."

Wait. What? Did I trade one type of bullying for another? FML

BALL & CHAIN

They sat across from each other on either side of the ballistic glass, rotary-style phone receivers in hand. He listened intently as he usually did during these weekly visits, and she did most of the talking.

"Time's up, inmate," said CO McNeil. "Wrap it up."

Sarah looked over her shoulder at him with a sarcastic, acknowledging grin.

"Charming guy," Charles said.

They pressed their hands up to the glass as they traditionally did at the end of these sittings.

"We'll be together soon enough," said Charles in an attempt to reassure her that their next appeal attempt would pan out, and they said their goodbyes.

CO McNeil re-shackled Sarah to lead her back to her cell.

Inside, after the steel door of her cell shut behind her, she stuck her hands through the opening she received her meals through, and those cold metal bracelets were released. Aside from Charles's tri-monthly visits, a daily shower, and an hour a day allowed for walking around in the prison yard...alone...this six-by-eight-foot cell was her world. The one book per week that she could order from the prison library and the reoccurring nightmares she'd have about her sentencing were her only company. You'd have thought she'd be batshit crazy by then. It had only been eight months since her sentencing, but that was about seven and a half months more than other inmates took to lose their shit. She wasn't shouting, being irrational, or acting out like the other lifers in this block though. She was actually a model inmate. There was an eerie calm about her. Like she was in on a joke that went over everyone else's head.

She flopped on her bunk and stared at the ceiling, reflecting on the judge's words again for the millionth time.

"Will the defendant please rise," said Judge Muhler. "Mrs. DeFranco, you stand here before us seemingly remorseful, but your endless stream of manipulative tears couldn't drown the sorrow these family members feel. They have lost a loved one by your hand. The fact of the matter is that four people lost their lives while another remains in a vegetative state. We have reason to believe beyond the shadow of a doubt that you poisoned your patients with the ricin that led to their eventual deaths. You plead ignorance, but I see deliberate malpractice. You plead inexperience, but I see malicious intent. I hereby sentence you to life in prison without the possibility of parole.

SHE'D BEEN RELIVING this moment almost every night, expecting a more lenient outcome each time, and would wake up in a cold sweat when she didn't get it.

ON HIS WAY HOME, Charles ran a few errands as he routinely did after visiting his incarcerated wife. Although the trips back home were shorter now after the move, it still seemed like a lot to leave behind—renting out the house he'd inherited after the brain aneurysm-induced seizure claimed his father's life three years prior, the staff accountant position at Wilton Capital, and the neighborhood he'd grown up in. He wasn't passionate about his work, but his job was actually enjoyable at times. Still, it was a bit much to give up for the sake of more frequent visitations. But he was in there with her, loyal to a fault (if there is such a thing). Self-less. Obedient, one might even say. Plus, Sarah rarely ever *didn't* get her way. She wanted him to reopen her bakery but closer to her. All he needed to find was a storefront, and she would teach him all her recipes during his visits. Life had revolved around her before. Why should it not now? Charles's world was now scheduled to exist outside and around every other Wednesday and the final Friday of each month. All the days in between were just fillers. His days now consisted of submitting appeal requests to reopen Sarah's case, consoling his incarcerated wife, and carrying out her wishes to make her happy.

Before this new reality, they'd led normal enough cookie-cutter lives. Charles was an accountant, and Sarah ran a small but thriving bakery in town. She was known for her complementary raspberry-drop sugar cookies that she indiscriminately gave away to anyone who asked, even nonpaying customers. Many a day, frustrated parents came in to yank their freeloading eight-year-olds out of the bakery. The kids would sneak away to get their sugar fix when the elementary school across the street let out for the day.

"Ms. Sarah! Ms. Sarah! Can I have a cookie?" they would ask excitedly.

"Okay, but just one more. I wouldn't want you to ruin your supper," she responded while giving them a playful wink.

She was loved. Even the aggravated parents would take one of these delicious bite-sized sugar cookies to go when they came to get their kids. Most of the parents, school staff, and faculty were regular customers. All birthday cakes and bunches of cupcakes to reward a class for good behavior were purchased at Ms. Sarah's Bakery. Business was good, and she was happy doing what she did. She was much happier than when she'd worked at the hospital.

Charles, on the other hand, didn't *hate* his nine-to-five, but he didn't *love* it either. After work, he would clock in a couple more hours per week, taking care of the financials for Sarah's Bakery—pro bono, of course—but this he loved. It gave him a sense of purpose, and he was great at it too. Meticulous like no other. Sarah was an amazingly artsy baker, but the business wouldn't have been "in the green" without Charles's oversight.

In about two months' time, with the savings they'd scraped together, the rental income from Charles's father's home, and a part-time gig as an adjunct accounting professor over at the local community college, PACC, he leased out a storefront. Her determination and his tenacity were making the dream of Sarah's Bakery II come to fruition. It was about a quarter of the size of the original but meant the world to her. Her happiness was his main priority, so he shared in her elation. On that Wednesday, she gave him detailed instructions for what equipment to order and paint, decoration, and general organization. It turned out to be a cozy little bakery, a mini replica of its predecessor. In just under three weeks, he brought pictures in to press up against the bulletproof glass. She loved it! Charles learned a couple of her muffin recipes (corn & blueberry) and a handful of recipes for assorted cookies that same day.

After the grand opening, business wasn't what you would call booming, but it was doing rather nicely in their new, less densely populated location. Charles estimated they should turn a profit inside of six months. He had this strange quirk about not tasting anything he baked, but his baking wasn't half bad. Who would've thought?

"When are you going to teach me the sugar cookie recipe?" he asked. "I think they'll be a hit again."

"In time, hun. And I know they'll be," she responded. "I just don't want that to be the primary reason customers are coming in this time. We need to win them over first...and we will."

They were both right. Midway through month four, Sarah's Bakery II was in the green, barely covering all of its costs but building up a loyal client base and turning a small profit.

"It's time to debut our raspberry-drop sugar cookies, babe. And I'm so proud of you, by the way. You're doing a great job!" she told Charles.

"*We're* doing a great job, babe," he corrected her. "You know this doesn't exist without you. So tell me how to you make those delicious bites of bliss."

"You can't be upset with me," she told him.

"Upset? Why would I be upset?" Charles asked.

"Because I never told you about my secret stash," she said, "but I couldn't afford to let my recipes get out. I never told a soul."

"Okay," he said shortly and with a surprised look on his face. "Where is it?"

Sarah explained she had locked away certain recipes, along with some rare ingredients (some spices and sugars imported from overseas) in a storage garage a few miles from their old home.

Charles was definitely surprised and upset. This type of deception made him livid. But given the circumstances, he let it go.

Following her direction, he was able to retrieve the key to this secret location from an unused old mailbox behind the shed of their old home. He went to the twenty-four-hour access storage place a few miles away and located her lot, 109. It looked like those little garages you see on reality shows like *Storage Wars*. He opened it up and went inside.

It was pretty well organized. You could tell she frequented it fairly often. There were a few shelves with color-coded, unlabeled bottles and jars on them. Some were filled with a sugary-like substance, and others looked to have a flour-like texture. There was a desk and a small filing cabinet where she apparently safeguarded her recipes. He was taken-a-back by some of the medical supplies she had there. Finding stethoscopes, scrubs, syringes, and boxes of latex gloves, he wrote it off as supplies she'd taken from her hospital gig before starting to bake full time. But how long had she been hiding this place then? It had been a long day filled with information he was still processing, so he called it a night and went home to get some rest. Tomorrow would be another day.

Charles was upset about Sarah's secret place but knew he could never stay mad at her. Still, on his next visit (the final Friday of the month visit), he let her know he wasn't going to make it to the next one. She knew his passive-aggressiveness all too well and, without skipping a beat, told him what he needed to hear in order to go through the motions of his little revolt a bit faster. She pouted and batted her ocean blue eyes at him and, in an innocent little girl voice, asked, "Why, baby?"

"Because the fall semester starts in two weeks and orientation is a bit earlier than usual. With most of my time dedicated to your bakery—"

"*Our* bakery," she corrected in that same manipulative voice.

He continued, "I haven't been able to put a lesson plan together yet."

Sarah gave him a sad face through the double-pane glass, and Charles cut his eyes away in dissent.

"I'm so proud of you, baby," she told him. "You're juggling so much. I'd be lost without you. You have other responsibilities and can't just focus on keeping me happy. I'll miss you terribly, but I understand."

"I'll definitely be here for the next Wednesday visit afterward, though," he assured her.

"I knew you wouldn't break my heart for too long, baby," she replied. "Just remember that you're mine. These kids are lucky to borrow you."

"I know, hun," he replied. "And you're all mine."

"That's right!" she said, smiling back. "I hate them for taking you away from me, but I want you to make a good impression on your first day. Let's make them a batch of the sugar cookies."

"Think I'm ready to make those?" he asked.

"I know you are. My baby can do anything he sets his mind to." A little ego stroking hurt no one, right? "Okay, I've always made two different types. They taste similar enough, but one uses more of the high-end imported ingredients and is only for special occasions. The other is just as good but less costly to make. Let's make your new students the special batch," she said.

She went on to meticulously explain the two different recipes, having him repeat each one to her several times to make sure he knew the right combination of color-coded jars.

"Okay, I got it," he said, frustrated.

"I'm sowwy," she said. "You know how important these cookies are to me."

"Yea, I know," he replied.

"Lastly, my filing cabinet has some paperwork I need you to mail in to the DA for me. I told my public defendant about it, but you know how they all but ignore appeal requests for cases they feel they can't win," she said.

"Okay, sure. What's in it?" he asked.

"Just some information I put together before my trial that I never gave the attorney. But maybe it can help with the appeal request. There are two thick manila envelopes already sealed and ready to go. One is a copy and says copy on it, just so I could keep track of what I already submitted, so you just have to mail in the one," she replied.

"Time's up, inmate," chimed in CO McNeil.

"I'm on it, hun, I'll make you proud. Promise," Charles replied, and they said their goodbyes.

CO McNeil put the cuffs on and led Sarah back to her cell as always. She stopped in front of her cell and turned to face him before walking in, making sure her straight blonde hair brushed his face as she spun around.

"I see the way you look at me, McNeil," she told him as she stared raptly into his eyes.

"What are you talking about, inmate? Go into your cell," he said.

He did check her out, though. All the guards did. Visitors did too. She was easily the most attractive woman in the prison, the type of woman who would own a room just from walking into it.

"Yes, sir," she told him. "I'll do *anything* you say," she said salaciously as she moved half a step into his personal space.

He cracked half a smile.

She reached down with both hands, still in handcuffs, and gently grabbed onto the now-obvious bulge in his blue pants. "Oooh," she said with a seductive rasp in her voice as she fondled him for a bit. "You know, you could do whatever you wanted to me if it weren't for all these cameras around." She licked and bit her bottom lip, then let go and took a step backward into her cell.

CO McNeil didn't say a word as he slid the red steel door shut.

She poked her hands out through the door's opening and he removed the restraints, caressing her hands before letting go and closing the opening.

On his way home, Charles passed by the storage unit to pick up what Sarah had told him he needed for the cookies and also grabbed the manila envelope to be mailed. The day before orientation, he followed her instructions precisely and made a large batch of raspberry-drop sugar cookies. They were a hit at orientation. Most of the students in the lecture hall took one on the way in and another on the way out. He thought the treat may have even distracted some of them from taking part in the usual rumors, but he still overheard a few of the students on their way out after class.

"Did you know his wife is in jail?! I heard she killed kids or something."

"Yea, I know, but I heard she was insanely jealous and caught him cheating with a student, and she killed her!"

"Hmm, I think I'll flirt my way to an A then." They giggled and laughed.

"You're both wrong. I looked up some old newspapers last semester in the library, from around the time it happened. She was fired from being a nurse at a local hospital where they used to live. They said it was negligence or something. Then, months after, they investigated and found that three or four of the patients who died under her watch were actually poisoned."

"Holy shit. Are you serious?"

"Yup, you can look it up too."

"Wow, what a sick bitch."

This was actually less commotion about his wife than he was used to overhearing, so all in all, it was a good day. He grabbed his messenger bag and noticed he never mailed Sarah's evidence for the appeal. On his way off campus, he passed by the main office and tossed it in with the outgoing mail batch.

In the days that followed, a few flirty looks and winks were shared between the inmate and CO, but aside from that, it was business as usual at the Muncy DOC. Charles missed the next Wednesday visit as expected but was predictably already on the visitors' list for the third Wednesday of the month.

Soon enough it was visiting Wednesday again, and Charles approached the double-pane glass eagerly waiting for Sarah to walk through the double door that separated the visiting area from the housing units. Inmates and visitors filled the room along with measured levels of mixed emotions. She walked in and locked eyes with him instantly as she approached him with an ear-to-ear smile. He lit up like HIDs with the phone already up to his ear. She sat down and picked up the phone on her side:

"Hey, stranger," she said playfully.

"Hey, you. I've missed you," he cooed.

"How'd your orientation go?" she asked.

"It went great! And your cookies were a hit. On a different note, though, I heard murmurs of the usual rumors," he told her.

"It's okay," she responded.

After their visit, CO McNeil led Sarah back to her cell as he normally did. This time when they got to the front of her cell, he grabbed her waist on either side and pressed himself up behind her. She welcomed it with a flirty moan.

He took in a deep breath of her essence and then whispered into her ear right before he nibbled on her neck, "I disabled that camera up there. Put in a work order for it, which won't be looked at until the Sunday after next. What was it you were saying about me doing anything I wanted with you?"

Sarah turned around to face him with a mischievous smile on her face. She used both hands, since they were still cuffed, to grab McNeil by the belt and pull him into the cell with her. They spent the next fifteen minutes of privacy quenching the pent-up sexual frustration they'd been flirting with for weeks. By Saturday night, there were at least half a dozen of these visits, mixed in with plotting and scheming.

"Are you sure the evidence you had him submit is

enough?" he asked as he zipped up his pants and she wiped her mouth.

"I'm positive. There's so much self-incriminating information in there that he should be arrested before next week is out, and I'll be released pending his prosecution," she replied.

"That could take weeks. Months even," he said. "What if I can't wait that long?"

"Be patient, baby," she told him. "We'll be together in increments longer than fifteen minutes soon enough."

"I have a better idea. We'll stage an attack of you on me," he explained. "My carelessness coupled with your cunningness would make for a believable escape."

"What about your job? You can't be on the run with me," she said.

"That won't be an issue," he replied. "With the union on my side, the most that will happen is a fine and/or suspension. Then by the time they arrest him, they'll be so eager to sweep your escape under the rug that they'll acquit you of all charges and streamline his sentencing."

"I love a man who can take charge the way you do," she agreed.

They settled on Friday during her yard time. He came back later that evening before his shift was over and they hammered out an outline. By Thursday night, they had every angle measured and every wrinkle of doubt ironed out.

Friday morning routinely came and went.

When the sun fell midway down the sky, McNeil went over to Sarah's cell to escort her outside. As he loosely placed the bracelets around her wrists without securing them in place, he told her, "Remember what I told you. Don't crawl back into the car until after I go back in to ring the alarm. It's very important that I follow protocol. Stay low to the ground, then wedge yourself between the back seat and the trick trunk I told you about. Just pull down that yellow strap to open it up. They *will* search my vehicle, so don't make a sound or move around until I let you out. This could take *hours*."

"Sir, yes, sir," she said playfully.

They walked out to the yard as they normally did. McNeil unlocked the gate that led to the employee parking lot to "get a pack of smokes" from his red '02 Mustang. On cue, Sarah loosened her cuffs, wrapped one around her fist like brass knuckles, and clocked CO McNeil twice while his back was turned, drawing blood from the back of his head. Then she ran off into the three-miles of forest opposite the parking lot.

McNeil eventually sat up and stumbled through the mess hall with blood trickling down his ear and neck, into the CO control room to sound the alarm. "Inmate escape, inmate escape," he repeated out of breath in an Oscar-worthy performance.

The other correction officers fell in line, following the proper protocol to begin the search.

There were failed escape attempts at Muncy quarterly. Some stressed-out inmate would try to climb the fence or get boosted over a wall. But it would always end the same way. The dogs would sniff them out of the bush, and they'd spend a month in the hole. Not this time though. By the time Warden Glenn came down to give the search order and speak with McNeil about what happened, Sarah had safely crawled into the back of the Mustang, entering from the far side, away from the camera, and wedged herself into the concealed compartment that was scent proof. McNeil had purchased the car at the PAPD Repo Auction, and the previous owner had been an "importer/exporter." After an exhaustive search that yielded no results, including the thorough search of all the employee vehicles in the lot, Warden Glenn interrogated CO McNeil one last time while the prison nurse finished applying eight stitches to his head.

"The media are going to have a field day with this! How could you be so fucking careless?" Warden Glenn yelled.

"She attacked me, boss," McNeil replied. "I didn't even see it coming."

"By a woman half your damn size, that *you* failed to properly inspect and secure," Warden Glenn rebutted.

"I inspected and secured the inmate. I do not know what she hit me with," CO McNeil replied. "A rock maybe?"

"A rock wouldn't cause a wound this narrow and deep," Nurse Kelly chimed in.

"Regardless, this happened on your watch. You can't be trusted to do your job properly right now, and we need to show a swift response to this situation for when the media gets a hold of it," said Warden Glenn.

"I understand, boss," McNeil replied remorsefully.

"You're suspended for a month without pay effective immediately. Upon your reinstatement, you'll go into two weeks of the inmate protocol refresher training, also without pay. Understood?" the Warden said.

"Yes, sir," replied CO McNeil, "and again, I'm sorry."

By the time he finished that sentence, Warden Glenn had already walked out of the room.

After gathering a few things from his locker, he went out to his car, opened up the trunk, and placed the box inside. After closing the truck, he got in, started the car, and went off as he normally did. After clearing the guard at the

Muncy entrance, he pulled over so he could go back and speak to Sarah.

"Babe?" he said aloud.

"I was beginning to think you forgot about me," Sarah replied jokingly.

"Do you need anything?" he asked. "I'm sure they'll be a checkpoint farther ahead and we can't risk a camera spotting you, so I can't let you out until we get to my apartment."

"No, I'm fine," she replied.

There was a checkpoint about a quarter mile after the forestry surrounding the prison. McNeil approached, slowed, and lowered his window.

"How's it going, Torres?" he greeted the officer who had signaled him to stop.

"McNeil...tough one today, huh?" Torres replied.

"Yea, you won't be seeing me around for a while," McNeil replied, fishing for sympathy.

"They finally get rid of you?" Torres said jokingly.

"Ha, not that easily, man. A month and a half, no pay," McNeil replied.

"Ouch!" Torres said. "Keep your head up, buddy. Shit happens."

"Thanks, man. Good night," he replied.

They made it to the apartment unnoticed and laid low for a few days. She changed her appearance and was now a short-haired brunette. Between their *Fifty Shades of Gray*-ish sexcapades, they watched television while waiting on breaking news of the escape to materialize...but it never did. The Muncy DOC was under code-red lockdown, which meant no one in or out. They had a skeleton staff housed on premises for a few days and kept every inmate caged 24/7.

They searched for news online, and nothing. Sarah also

accessed Charles's emails and read through some of the flirty emails he had going back and forth with a student (Amy Lessig) who was in search of some one-on-one tutoring. She recognized the address Charles gave Amy from the return address on the holiday cards he had sent her in the past.

Right before dawn on the fourth day after her escape, and on the day her grand plan, years in the making, would finally come to fruition, Sarah took the Mustang and drove over to the storage facility, using the key she'd stashed close by. Next, she went to Charles's apartment.

Charles woke up and made his way into the kitchen for a glass of tap water. He looked worried as he stared out the window above the sink, like he hadn't gotten enough sleep.

Having already made her way into the apartment, Sarah slid up behind him and injected him Dexter style.

He felt the piercing pinch of the syringe needle on the right side of his neck. About thirty minutes later he came to, his vision slowly clearing enough for him to evaluate his surroundings. His arms and legs were zip-tied to one of his dining room chairs and his mouth was duct-taped. Next to him, Amy was similarly secured but not yet conscious.

Sarah sat on top of the island in the kitchen, looking down on them. "So who's this? The student of the month?" she said sarcastically. "You selfish son of a bitch. Is this what you've been doing while I've been suffering alone? You should be ashamed of yourself. You told me you changed. You told me Beth was the last one." She cocked her head at him as he tried to plead with her. "What? You want to explain?"

Beth had been a coworker of Charles's who he'd had an affair with back at Wilton Capital. After snooping through his credit card statements and emails, Sarah had pieced it all together and pretty much caught him red-handed. After a brief separation, Sarah wound up forgiving and consoling Charles when she found out that had Beth died suddenly of liver and lung failures.

Sarah hopped down off the counter, walked over to Charles, and yanked the duct tape off his mouth in one fluid motion that almost took his lips.

He yelled, "Owwww, fuck! What the hell did you do to her?" Turning to his student, he pleaded, "Amy! Amy, wake up!"

"Oh, I'm sorry. Amy can't come to the phone right now," Sarah said.

"What did you do, Sarah?" Charles continued. "Amy!"

"She can't hear you, asshole," Sarah said. "What I injected you with was a nap. What *she* got... Well, let's just say it's a bit more permanent than that. That slutty cunt won't ever hear you again."

"I can't fucking believe you. You're a monster. The cops are going to find you. I know everything. I won't keep my mouth shut, you crazy bitch," Charles said defiantly. "What are you even fucking doing here? How are you *here* right now?!"

"News flash, cheating Charlie, I'm out of prison... permanently. Besides, they didn't find out why a perfectly healthy Beth suddenly had health problems, did they?" she asked sarcastically, followed by a maniacal smirk.

Charles gasped in disbelief.

She walked around behind him and slid her hands down the front of his chest, then leaned in and whispered into his ear, "And your fathers' aneurysm...that was me too." She placed the duct tape over his mouth again as he squirmed and screamed and cried about what he had just learned.

"Let me tell you exactly what's going to happen here," Sarah began. "Within the next few hours, you'll wake up surrounded by cops who have a warrant for your arrest based on an anonymous call from yours truly. They'll read you your rights and book you. It will soon enough come to light via the manila envelope that you mailed in for me that *you* are responsible for each of the deaths they convicted me for. You met me at the hospital for lunches within three days of each of the deaths of my patients...remember that? You used me to finagle connections at the hospital behind my back, to get the ricin and syringes that you used.

"It was a shame about poor Beth too. She was tired of being the other woman and was going to expose you and your affair. There's the motive for her unexplained death. Should I continue?

"Did you notice your class size go down for a bit after cookie day? That's because you began experimenting on students by dosing them with nonfatal amounts of ricin. Oh, wait, but there's nothing here in the apartment linking you to any of this, right? That's right...you also gave them the location of the storage facility you've been going to fairly often, which has syringes like these and dozens of containers with different levels ricin doses. And the best part? *Your* fingerprints, and only your fingerprints, are all over the place. And little Amy here, her death will be the cherry on top for them to build their case. As for me, it won't matter that I've slipped out of jail a bit sooner than expected. It'll all be swept under the warden's rug."

∾

Over at Muncy, Warden Glenn was on the phone with the district judge. "I'm calling in that favor, Terrence," the warden said.

"Again?" the judge replied. "How much leverage do you think you have with me exactly?"

"Enough to make this phone call. And trust me, the alternative would be worse for all of us. All I need is a signed arrest warrant and your word on a swift, no-jury sentencing," said the warden.

"Even if I was willing to cut through the red tape to expedite this, you know I can't give you an arrest warrant without PC," the judge replied.

"I'm looking at all the PC you'll ever need as we speak. I have a full confession letter along with corroborating evidence we've already checked out and confirmed," said Warden Glenn.

"Okay, so why not go through the proper channels?" the judge asked.

"It's better you not know," replied the warden.

"I'm not sure what you think I owe you for introducing me to your buddy with the underground casino and massage joints, but it's definitely not enough to get you a blank check in the form of an arrest warrant. So tell me, what's the urgency about?" the Judge said.

"Judge, there was an escape a few days ago," the warden said.

"A successful one?" the surprised judge asked.

"Yes. Remember the nurse that killed a handful of patients last year? Her. But with the husband's confession and the evidence pointing to him, he's taking the wrap for all of it and more."

"And you buy this bullshit?" the judge asked. "Seems convenient."

"Belief isn't a requisite of my job, Judge. If it checks out, it checks out. She'll be released, he'll be sentenced, and nobody will be the wiser."

"Okay, Glenn, you have a verbal arrest warrant granted. If this blows up in your face, I won't back up or document this though."

"Don't worry, Judge," Warden Glenn replied. "We'll clean this up on our end. Soon you can go back to your table games and happy endings, stress free. Oh, and Terrance?"

"Yes?"

"Give my best to Marie and the twins," the warden said before hanging up.

BACK AT THE APARTMENT, Sarah grabbed a fistful of Charles's hair and yanked it back. They locked eyes.

"You did this to us. Don't you forget that," she told him as she leaned in and kissed him on the lips over the duct tape.

She squeezed out a few drops from the syringe and then flicked it and shot it into his neck. "Sleep tight, baby," she whispered.

She tied Amy's wrists to the headboard in the bedroom to make it look like an intense sex scene gone awry. She made sure his fingerprints were on the ricin needle, then she vanished.

Charles came to as his apartment was being raided for his arrest. He tried to explain, but they saw it as resisting and clubbed the back of his knees, dropping him to the ground, and then they cuffed him.

EIGHT MONTHS LATER, Charles lay on a cot in a cell not dissimilar to the one Sarah was once in, reading *The Count of Monte Cristo* as a prison guard approached.

"DeFranco, you have a visitor," said the guard.

But Charles didn't respond.

"DeFranco!" he said as he pulled out his club and banged it against the cell bars.

"I heard you the first time, Jimenez. I'm trying to read here," he replied.

"It's not a request, you smug asshole," said Jimenez. "In ten minutes, you'll be escorted to the visitors' room."

Charles thought it was another reporter or attorney trying to make a name for themselves with a high-profile appeal case, albeit an unwinnable one but in the public eye nonetheless. Boy, was he wrong.

As he walked into the visitors' room, the CO on duty chimed in, "Your visitor is hot as fuck, by the way."

"Oh yea?" Charles replied, uninterested.

"Yea, you miserable prick," the CO said.

Charles signed into the room and walked over to window nine where a redheaded woman with big sunglasses sat on the opposite side. He knew who it was in the depths of his soul before his brain even finished processing. As he sat down and picked up the phone, she removed her glasses. Her piercing blue eyes unapologetically stared back at him.

"You heartless bitch! I could kill you," Charles spat at the window.

"Oh, Charlie, so much aggression. Haven't you done enough killing already? What would your father think if he saw you this way?"

"You're a sick and evil person. How do you have the gall to show your face?" Charles said.

"I just didn't want you to worry about me, darling. I wanted to let you know I sold the house and am moving to Florida," Sarah stated.

"What?! My father's house? You didn't. You couldn't," Charles said in disbelief.

"*My* house actually. Remember how transferring the deed into my name would benefit my appeal? Well, it did," she said mockingly. "I'm leaving tomorrow, just wanted to say goodbye, Charlie. Make sure you sit and think about what you've done to me and if any of those other women were worth it."

She hung up the phone, stood and blew him a kiss, then put on her glasses and walked out of his life forever.

Charles had become livid beyond anything he'd ever felt before, yelling and screaming, slamming and breaking the phone against the glass. "You fucking bitch! Come back here! Come back here!"

The guard ran over after calling it in on his walkie-talkie. Charles nailed him with a right hook to the jaw, which caught the guard by surprise but only stunned him for a split second. The guard pulled out his club and jammed it into Charles's stomach and then elbowed him in the nose. Two other guards rushed in and helped wrestle Charles to the ground while he continued thrashing and screaming.

"It was her! She was here! It wasn't me, God damn it! Listen to me!" he yelled out in rage and pain.

The nurse was called and came in with a syringe that they used to sedate him.

Charles woke up in a slightly larger room, restrained to an unfamiliar bed. The time that had lapsed in between was a mystery to him. Had it been hours? Weeks? Months?

He couldn't recall a thing between then and now. But he picked up where he left off.

"It was her! She was here! It wasn't me! Let me out. Let me out of here!" he slurred.

A nurse turned to the doctor in charge of this psych ward for instruction.

"Continue to sedate him as long as these hallucinations continue," the doctor stated.

"Yes, Doctor," she replied.

As she approached Charles to sedate him, all he was able to say before things went dark again was, "Don't you stick me with that. I need to go to Florida. Let me out. It was her! It was really her. She needs to be stop—"

Hours later on Interstate 64, a redheaded woman was spotted alone at the wheel of a Red 2002 Mustang, flowing carefree through the traffic on her way to Florida with all that she needed in the trunk and some of what she no longer had use for in a scent-proof compartment.

CHOPPER CITY

It was a Saturday afternoon. A nice day too. Sunny but not too hot, and a cool, refreshing breeze blew at welcoming times. We were walking down Rockaway Boulevard by the new casino.

"Have you been there?" Dave asked me.

"Once," I replied. "How about you?"

"Nah, I haven't. I always lose when I gamble," he said.

"When do you ever gamble?" I asked.

"Like when I buy lottery tickets. Scratchy tickets and shit. Stuff like that, you know?" he said.

"Oh, please," I said. "That's hardly the same thing. You actually have to think in these places. Put some thought into the games and try to beat them."

"Oh, really? How much did you *beat* them for?" he asked.

"I lost twenty bucks," I admitted.

He burst out in laughter, then asked, "What happened to thinking and all that jazz?"

"I didn't say I *beat* them, dick. But that's what people in the know say. People who know their shit and play poker for a living."

"Yea, yea, Galileo. How was the place, though?"

"It was alright, I guess. A casino. I just walked around the main floor for a bit, didn't explore too much, but it was decent," I told him.

"Cool. We should go back. Are you down to go tonight?" he asked.

"Nah, I can't. I have plans with my girl already," I said.

"So they have twenty-dollar tables? Or ten dollars?" Dave asked.

"I have no idea," I replied.

"What did you play then?" he asked, confused.

"Some nickel slots," I said.

And almost as if it were as involuntary as a leg extension during a patellar reflex test, he burst out into unmeasured laughter. In between breaths, he was able to muster, "You were giving me shit about scratchy tickets and you're over there playing nickel slots like a seventy-two-year-old lady who took a break from knitting?! Give me a break! You great thinker, you."

"Yea, fuck you too, dick. My point is still valid," I said, although I doubt he heard my response under his whaling laugh.

The only reason that laughter stopped was because of the loud noises and commotion we heard behind us. It wasn't the usual New York-type of loudness. It was a what-the-fuck-is-going-on, we're-in-this-together type of loudness. A cacophony of unfamiliar sounds sprinkled with people shouting and screaming that kept getting louder. And whatever it was, was flying in the sky and fast approaching. And then it was hovering directly above us. It looked like a cross between a fatigued-out military tank and an Apache helicopter.

Dave and I stood there, paralyzed by fear and general awe. By this point, we were directly across the street from the casino parking lot, in front of the entrance to the Hilton, which readily housed pilots and stewardesses who were between flights from JFK. This entire episode seemed like something out of a movie. I didn't know if I should run or take out my iPhone and start recording. The suspense didn't last long before we heard a clear but accent-rich voice pierce through some sort of speaker system coming from the chopper.

"Every one of you is guilty!" exclaimed the angry voice. "From the CEO of each airline, to their board of directors, down to the laborers that allow themselves to be exploited by working for measly wages." His voice seemed to get increasingly frustrated and agitated as he continued. "From every citizen that uses your overpriced and oppressive services to every pilot doing their bidding. Collectively, you're all symptoms of the same diseased system! With a heavy heart, I will be the cure..."

During the next suspense-filled thirty-second or so pause, a larger crowd gathered while some quickly fled the scene. Approaching fire engine and police cruiser sirens got louder as they got closer to the scene. What happened next was something straight out of a *Call of Duty* video game. The chopper shifted and some side compartment opened up. A portion of the metallic side rolled up like a garage door, exposing what was easily the biggest, most futuristic cannon of a gun that I had ever seen.

Within moments, sound-barrier-breaking bullets pierced the air and exploded through the glass exterior of the hotel. Glass shattered and flew toward us with a similar velocity, breaking windows, puncturing tires, and denting fenders. People ran screaming, some hit by glass, and others collapsed to the ground with pools of blood increasing in diameter beneath them.

I could not hear a thing. Even though the automatic nonstop shooting was so loud I could feel the sound-wave ripples, everything went silent. The screams, shattering glass, people getting hurt and killed, cars peeling out to get away. All of it seen. All of it witnessed. None of it heard. The silence served as a cloak, shielding me from the harsh reality around me, but I never felt so vulnerable.

As I stood there motionless, Dave reached up with his left hand and tugged at my shorts, only half lifting his tucked down head to yell, "Get down here!" at me to join him behind the mint green Buick LeSabre we'd been leaning on.

And I did. "What the fuck, bro?! How are we going to get out of here?" I asked Dave.

"That crazy fuck seems to only have it in for this building. We'll be okay. We'll be okay. We need to wait it out here," he replied.

At that moment, the chopper stopped shooting and began shifting in its place with the long barrel of the gun pointed toward the people and cars in the street. After what must have been a reloading break, it began firing the gigantic cannon gun again. This time, the targets were random. Then the police cruisers we'd only heard so far were now visible but shot into oblivion as soon as they arrived. A couple of them instantly burst into flames as the officers ran out looking for cover. They drew their weapons as soon as they could crouch down behind something and fired at will. A noble attempt, but their bullets seemed like mosquitoes the chopper just shooed away.

Other cars and nearby buildings were hit too. Colorful lightbulb-covered awnings of surrounding businesses that looked like mini casinos themselves were getting picked off like empty beer and soda cans on a wooden fence in Texas. People were being slain. Bullets sliced through limbs like a rolling pizza knife. Innocent, defenseless women, children, seniors, and men, all gone. Shot down and killed in cold blood.

When all hope was lost and death seemed imminent to all of us who were left, we saw at a distance behind the chopper that five fighter jets were fast approaching in perfect triangulated form, completely in sync with one another. With no warning and zero hesitation, the lead jet unloaded rounds from the circular machine guns on either side under its wings. Most hit the target dead on with only a handful hitting the mostly evacuated grounds all around us. Almost instantly, two of the flanking jets separated from the triangular formation, dropped down, and went forward simultaneously, each shooting out a missile. The chopper, distracted by first chopper's barrage of bullets, was barely aware enough to react, and they two missiles each hit their target with unparalleled accuracy. The chopper, along with anyone and everyone on board it, exploded in the sky.

This time I heard it. Dave and I were both pinned down to the ground by the blast, but shielded from debris by the valiant Buick we hadn't strayed from.

Slowly bringing my head up from between my legs, I looked up from the fetal-like position I was in. It was a confusing moment. It seemed to have instantly gone from afternoon daylight to dusk. The entire sky rippled as if everything were under water. In the distance, I kept hearing someone call out, "Sanchez! Sanchez! Sanchez! Wake up, Jarhead. It's 0800. You're on watch duty. There was another drone strike in Datta Khel. We're moving out to go secure the area."

"Hoorah," I replied as I came back to my senses.

It had all been a dream... Well, being on *that* helpless, voiceless side of this mess was.

LECTURE HALL

"Will the Great Recession be on the midterm, Professor?" one student asked.

"Absolutely," replied the professor. "And here's the type of essay I'm looking for, folks. Show the understanding that the catalyst was the burst of the tech bubble in the early 2000s. People searched for safer investments and settled on real estate. In turn, home demands rose while supply fell. And what does that do to the price, class?"

"It drives it up," responded a student from the back of the lecture hall.

"Correct, whoever that was," the professor said. "It drives the price up, which artificially inflates home values. So what then? Houses across the nation are now "worth" more than ever before in recorded history. And here's where individual greed comes in. People owe less than what their homes are now artificially inflated to be worth. That spread between the value and what they owe is called *equity*. And what do they do? Instead of leaving well enough alone, they borrow against that equity. They buy other houses, cars, boats...luxury items they don't need. Greed is good, huh? Not in this case."

"But, Professor—" another student began.

"Hold on, David, let me finish this point first," the professor said. "As the spread continued to increase, some of these people took out second mortgages and lines of credit using their homes as ATMs. We were amid the next bubble, folks, and most of us didn't see it. Values kept going up, skyrocketing in some regions. But we missed the forest for the trees. Then Wall Street, which was fueled by their own greed, created financial instruments known as mortgage-backed securities. Think of them as stocks or bonds that comprised a collection of mortgages all bundled up and sold by the share to the general public. The thing is that these mortgage-backed securities weren't just made up of mortgages that were in good standing. They'd also include these doomed to fail subprime mortgages. They bundled them up together and sold them to the world. Infesting the globe.

"This leads to the next point that your essays should cover," he continued. "What exactly is the subprime mortgage market? Well, Wall Street wasn't satiated with the millions of dollars this market was generating. Nope. They wanted even more. Their greed needed to be fed. So the banks that you and I go to for a mortgage loosened up their guidelines for mortgage qualifications. This way, they'd have more mortgages on their books to feed Wall Street with. You no longer needed a 720 credit score...a 680 score would do. You didn't need 20 percent down plus closing costs...just come up with 10 percent plus closing costs. If you build it, they will come, and so they, the borrowers, came."

"But why is that the consumers' fault?" blurted out a student from the back of the lecture hall.

"Because there's something called personal responsibility, that's why!" replied the professor. "Nobody can exercise that for you. As I was saying, after the banks lowered mortgage qualifying requirements and Wall Street successfully sold off those securities, they lowered requirements even more. Soon you didn't need a down payment and closing costs weren't required either! They rolled up all of your costs into your mortgage loan. Can't pay for the appraisal out of pocket? Don't worry. We'll roll that cost in too.

"Some big banks like Countrywide, which to give you a bit of context—in 2006, Countrywide financed 20 percent of all mortgages in the United States at a value of about 3.5 percent of United States GDP—as well as a handful of lesser known, fly-by-night banks that popped up, even offered up to 106 percent financing. I'll say that again. One-hundred-and-six percent financing. That means that in some cases, they *paid* you to take out a mortgage! They paid *you* to buy a house! I shit you not. But we, the consumer, kept taking and taking and taking. Word to the wise, folks, if it seems too good to be true...it is! Questions? Comments?"

"I have a question," David said as he raised his hand.

"Go ahead, David," said Professor Nachman.

"You say that consumer greed is at the root of this issue, right?"

"Not just consumer greed," replied Professor Nachman, "but greed in general. Bank greed. Wall Street greed. Human greed. The blame goes all around."

"Well, I don't think I agree with you, Professor."

"Fair enough. Tell us why you don't," Professor Nachman said as he leaned on the front of his desk to listen.

"I guess greed plays into it," David continued. "A

general 'people wanting what they can't have' coupled with being told that they can now have all those things type of greed...but I wouldn't blame it solely on greed."

"There are absolutely other factors at play, young David, just none as strong or as underlying as greed," replied the professor.

"That's just it, I don't think everyone involved is necessarily being greedy. There's plenty to say about predatory lending. About lack of regulation, about manipulation and exploitation of a weak system," David added to make his point.

"David, if you're a minimum-wage worker at the local supermarket, for example, you should have the common sense to know you have no business purchasing a four-hundred-thousand-dollar home. And then, on top of that, an additional hundred-thousand-dollar line of credit against that same home, which you use to buy a new car and big screen TV. That's living beyond your means. That's exercising zero personal responsibility," the professor replied emphatically.

"But don't banks have a fiduciary responsibility to be truthful?" David replied. "Don't banks have a personal responsibility *not* to fuck over their customers?"

"Watch that tone and language in my classroom," the professor said.

"I'm sorry, Professor, it's just frustrating," David said. "My aunt, for example, came to this country twelve years ago. She worked ten- to twelve-hour days, six days a week, making sure my cousins never wanted for clothes on their backs or food in their stomachs. She even took me in for a year when my parents died in their accident. And she did it alone. But I guess she should have had the personal responsibility to pick a better husband, right?"

"What's your point, David?" asked the professor.

"The point is that she is a hard worker who scraped together her life savings of $10,000 to buy a house. She put all her eggs in one basket because that's all her local mortgage broker told her she needed," David replied. "She could finally fulfill the American dream for her and her family. He told her that her mortgage would be even less than she was currently paying in rent, because of an interest rate special he could get her for being a first-time homebuyer and for being a single, hardworking Latina woman. He even told her he could get her a line of credit for a new car too, but she didn't bite on that one. She got the house with only $10,000 down and they rolled closing costs into her new loan.

"He didn't tell her, however, about the several hundred dollars more per month that she would have to pay for PMI (Private Mortgage Insurance) because she didn't make a down payment of 20 percent. And of course he didn't mention the taxes and insurance, because everyone, including first-time homebuyers, should know that right? Instead, he misled her by quoting only the principal and interest payment and conveniently leaving out the rest. But it's okay. She's hardworking and knew things couldn't just go 100 percent smooth. Fine. She picked up a part-time job on Sundays to make ends meet. In her mind, working seven days a week is worth her children having a taste of the American dream. You want to know what he didn't tell her, though?"

"What's that?" the professor asked.

"That the type of loan he gave her was a six-month ARM," replied David. "She had an introductory teaser rate, meaning her interest rate and mortgage payment amount were locked in for only *six months*. Thereafter, it would more than double! She went back to the broker, thinking surely this had been some kind of mistake. He told her he'd look into it and strung her along, avoiding her calls for over two weeks. After that, when she showed up at his office again, he told her there was nothing he could do except refinance her into a thirty-year fixed rate loan, but it would cost her another $10,000 in closing costs and her *total* monthly payment would go down by only about $150. Long story short, the bank foreclosed and she lost the house. She lost it all. Now she's back in the Dominican Republic with her two kids. And her story is far from unique, by the way.

"What happened to the bank having a fiduciary responsibility to their customers? What happened to walking into making the biggest investment of your life and not having to worry about a snake-oil salesman taking you for a ride?"

"Let me ask you something, David. What happened to your aunt's personal responsibility?" the professor said. "What happened to your aunt knowing the limits of what she could afford? Folks...there are bad people out there. They'll always be there. We can't wrap the world in nerf material to help cushion the blow when we fall prey to bad actors. That's not how we win. We win by being accountable for our actions, for knowing what we're getting ourselves into."

"You're being disingenuous, Professor," David replied.

"Excuse me?" The professor sounded insulted.

"And unrealistic too. What you're saying makes sense for us, the younger generation. Those of us lucky enough to be learning this stuff in college. But what about my aunt? What about the immigrants that are preyed upon? What about the hardworking Americans even, that left school because they chose to nobly put their family's needs before their own and went to work in order to provide for them?

They obviously don't have the same information. So fuck them? Survival of the fittest, basically?"

"Watch your language in my classroom," replied Professor Nachman. "I won't tell you again."

"Sorry…I guess I just don't know any better," David replied. "But you know what, Professor? It shouldn't be okay to screw over the less fortunate and squeeze every dime out of them *just because you can*. And what's worse is that they continue to do so without repercussion. That's the issue. You say bad people will exist. Agreed. But we shouldn't have to write that off as the cost of doing business. Assholes need to be checked. Poor business practices, regulated. In a direct and unilateral way, attacking the root of the issue instead of hacking away at the symptomatic branches, to paraphrase Thoreau."

"Big government and regulation stifles progress and ingenuity," replied the professor. "There's a delicate balance that has to be struck there."

"Does it always?" David asked. "Can't it also allow progress and ingenuity to be free to thrive without corporate special interest intervention like the New Deal did with Social Security and other social programs after the Great Depression?"

"In the long run, the invisible hand prevails, and the markets balance themselves out," stated the professor. "So long as people remain content with knowing that ditch diggers and maids can't buy mansions."

"I agree with personal responsibility to a degree, but the underlying issue with this logic is that everyone can't know everything," David rebutted. "The maid who walks into a bank with her life savings shouldn't leave thinking she has a home just to find out six months later that she barely has a shirt on her back. And her children shouldn't have to decide between either breakfast *or* lunch because some unregulated banker wanted to add a diving board to the pool at his family's summer home."

"Tread lightly on that regulation slippery slope that you're on, David," the professor warned. "You may get exactly what you're asking for and live long enough to regret it in the future."

"Your generation doesn't get to tell ours what to do anymore," David replied defiantly.

"Okay, that's enough," said Professor Nachman.

"And it starts here, with this conversation," David added. "With doing what we can to help shift the collective consciousness into a space where we don't have a 'pass the buck' mob mentality. Where personal responsibility is balanced by unilateral repercussions. A dash of good old common sense could go a long way."

The bell rings, ending class.

ELEVATOR

"Honey, guess what?" Angela stated.

"What?" asked Daniel.

"You got another letter," she replied.

"Another rejection, you mean?" Daniel replied with a scowl.

"C'mon, don't say that. Be positive. Besides, I have a good feeling about this one." Angela smiled. "Here, open it." She handed him a letter that had come in the mail from one of the dozens of agents and publishing houses he'd submitted his latest manuscript to. Most of them had never responded.

"I guess you're right," Daniel said as he tore it open. "Maybe the sixteenth time is the charm, right?"

"Mommy?" their child's voice said from the other bedroom.

"Shoot. Let me go make sure he's okay," Angela said. "But open it, open it. I'll be right back."

Daniel slid the tri-folded letter out of the envelope and began to read as his heart rate elevated.

Friday, January 13th, 2017

Dear Author,

Thank you for the opportunity to consider your manuscript. We read it with interest, but I regret that we will not be making an offer of publication. We do not feel that it is the right fit for our publishing house.

Thank you for thinking of us, and we wish you every success in finding a publisher for your work. Keep on writing.

Yours sincerely,

Rough House

"He's fine. He just wanted his stuffed whale," Angela stated as she walked back into their bedroom. "So? What did they say?"

"They said that the seventeenth time might be the charm," responded Daniel, dejected.

"Awe, babe, I'm sorry. Come here," she said as she wrapped her loving arms over his shoulders and gave him a kiss. "I love your writing...and I hate reading, so if you can pull that off, they'll wise up eventually."

"Thanks, babe. I'm not sweating it. I mean, J. K. Rowling was rejected a dozen times before she got published."

"See, so no need to worry," Angela said.

"And Jack Canfield, who wrote the *Chicken Soup for the Soul* series had a whopping hundred and forty rejections."

"Let's try to keep it on the lower end of that spectrum," she said, smiling.

"I'm not worried," he replied. "It is what it is. I just need to work harder and get better."

"Good attitude, babe. Just make sure you don't beat yourself up, though. As it is, you wake up early, go to sleep late, and work weekends. You can't kill yourself either."

"What do you think about me writing full time?" Daniel asked.

"If we could afford it," Angela began, "that would be great. But we can't."

"I know we can't right now. I'm not just going to quit my job," Daniel reassured her. "I meant, if we actively save for it, plan for it."

"We barely make it out ahead of our mortgage and bills each month as is," Angela replied. "What are we going to save? Be realistic."

"I'm just sick of my job, Angela. So much that it's frustrating me to the point of affecting my writing time."

"So consider changing your job. I don't know, maybe get a job in something writing related. Or I can go back to work, but we discussed this. Most of my pay would go to the stranger who would be raising Carlos."

"I know, I know. I just feel like I have to get away from everything and really give it an honest go if I'm ever going to have a shot at making it," Daniel replied.

"We have a two-year-old in the other room and you're asking me this now? What are you running from?" Angela asked.

"What are you talking about? I'm not running from anything," Daniel responded, offended. "I'm still putting in fifty to sixty hours per week at work, aren't I? It just feels like I'm climbing two rungs up and one down the corporate ladder. And you know how I feel about writing full time. How I've always felt about it."

"And you know I've always supported your dreams," Angela reassured. "Even during all the nights and weekends when I felt I didn't exist while you were typing away our companionship. But this is different. We have a baby now. You can't just quit your job to follow some dream. Be real."

"Some dream?" Daniel asked. "First of all, the writing in and of itself is my dream, yes, but what I'm striving for is *ours*. More family time. The independence to live where we want. Travel when we want. And best of all, not having to rely on some corporation that utilizes me no differently than a copier uses its paper tray. I'm a functional piece of equipment in human form. You know this isn't just coming out of the blue. I've been doing the responsible thing and burning the candle on both ends for years."

"I know, and I've been with you every step of the way, remember? All I'm saying is that your timing bringing it up now just couldn't be more wrong," Angela said.

"There will always be reasons not to do it. Reasons I shouldn't start writing full time. And I won't do this if you're not on board, but think about it. How much longer should I keep letting those reasons win?" Daniel reasoned.

"What if you don't make it, or if your sales don't go up? What then?" Angela asked. "Is it worth not being able to put food in your baby's mouth? How about the health insurance? We can't be impulsive about this, Daniel."

"Since when do you know me to be impulsive?" Daniel asked. "I never said I was going to quit next week. Just that I wanted to gear up and plan for doing so. We have to work all the angles out beforehand. As far as medical coverage, we can go on public insurance. We have a bit of savings too. I'm not saying it would be easy, but there are answers. Alternatives. They may take six months or a year, or even more, to establish. Just think about it, will ya? I gotta go. I'm running late. We'll speak about it more at dinner." He leaned in and gave her a kiss goodbye.

"I don't think there's anything to think about," she said.

"Don't be irrational," he replied. "We'll speak later tonight. I love you."

Daniel left and walked the four blocks that began his hour-long journey from home to the bus, then to the train that took him into his nine-to-five in the city.

Back home, his wife watched cartoons with the baby and focused in on a bit of dialogue.

"I don't ever want to be a grownup!"

"Why is that, Molly?"

"They never have time to have fun! It's always work, work, work. And when they're not working, they're too tired to play with me!"

"Well, Molly, grownups have to work so they can be able to feed you, clothe you, and buy you the toys you want. One day you'll be a grownup and you'll enjoy working to provide for your kids. That's what family's all about."

Some playful background music chimed in as Molly broke out into a song and dance routine.

"Being a grownup isn't always what it seems. When I grow up, I'm gonna dream. Having to work is overrated, so when I grow up, I'm gonna dream.

We're going to play all day and enjoy or snacks, and even look forward to taking naps! When I grow up, I'm gonna dreeeam. And I'll never lose sight of what it means."

"You know what, Molly? You might be right. Maybe it wouldn't be so bad if grownups dreamt every once in a while."

Angela looked at her baby boy and asked, "You're going to follow your dreams, aren't you, Carlito?"

Daniel missed his stop on the train because it was so packed that, by the time he looked up from the notebook he was writing in, he couldn't get to the door on time before more people rushed in and the doors closed behind them. During rush hour, if you're not strategically positioned within the train car, you have to develop quartz-like timing, along with an elite acrobatic ability to get past the bookbags, baby strollers, and people who either aren't paying attention or just don't give a fuck that they're in the way.

After a long day of work that included an unpaid hour of overtime, about four cups of coffee, the deli giving him the wrong overpriced sandwich for lunch (he hates chicken salad), and his shirt ripping on the elbow from rubbing it on his desk, he headed home. The subway platform was so full when he got there that he had to stand halfway up the staircase and just wait until enough trains passed by to alleviate the congestion. Four trains came and went by the time he was close enough to squeeze into the crowded fifth one. There he was, stuck between a teenager blasting some God-awful music through his headphones and a mouth breather with subpar personal hygiene. The train stopped on five separate occasions in between stations due to "train traffic ahead." He eventually made it above ground and to his stop. He checked his phone, finding his wife had texted him.

"Everything okay, babe?"

He replied, "Yea. Train was packed and delayed, though. Just got above ground. About to wait for the bus. Start eating dinner without me. Love you."

Angela waited for him to arrive and then warmed up dinner for both of them while Daniel settled in and spent time with Carlos. Even though he insisted, she never liked eating alone.

"Dinner's ready," she said.

"Let's go eat, buddy," Daniel told Carlos. "Then we'll play, okay?"

"Okay, Daddy," Baby Carlos replied.

Carlos hopped up and into his highchair as they sat at the dinner table.

"Long day, huh?" Angela said.

"Yea, babe, but it is what it is," Daniel began. "The train was just OD backed up. You should've seen that platform. It was like a sea of people. I literally had to stand on the stairs and wait for it to be empty enough for me to get closer."

"Damn, I'm sorry, hun," she replied sympathetically.

"Dinner looks great though. Thanks, sweetie," Daniel told her. "Eat your food, buddy. If not, then no playtime."

"I was thinking about what you said earlier, Danny," said Angela.

"Yea, me too, and you're right. I'm sorry I even brought it up," Daniel replied.

"No, I'm glad you did. Don't be sorry about that. We should always be able to speak our minds and express what we're feeling to each other. No matter what. Warts and all. If we can't be vulnerable with each other, then who can we be that open with?"

"Yea, I guess," Daniel replied. "But it is way too risky of a thing to think about now. Maybe when Carlos goes into school and if you decide to go back to work, maybe then we can revisit it. In the meantime, I'll focus on getting better. Quality can't be denied. That's where my focus needs to be right now."

"That is a way to go, but if you want to figure something out, I'm with you, babe," Angela said. "We could cut back on everything for a while, like dinners and movies, save up a few months' worth of bills, and then give it a shot.

Or any other way that we can make it happen sooner. I won't ever be able to forgive myself for stopping you from chasing down your dream. And I know you could do it. Without a doubt, I do. I support you and will do anything I can on my part because, like you said, it'll lead to our dream life and, more importantly, it'll show Carlito that he can truly be anything he wants to be."

"I really appreciate that, sweetheart," he replied. "But honestly, the more I thought about it, the more I agreed with what you said this morning. I mean, you know the responsible side of me wouldn't do it without having an established ironclad backup plan and nest egg. The thing is that, in a worst-case scenario situation, which is what I believe we'd have to plan for, what if it doesn't work out and I can't get a job when I need to? I can't put you or Carlito in that situation. I was thinking, and if I wake up a half hour earlier than I am already and wake up just as early on the weekends, I'll be able to write that much more per week. The more I write, the better I'll get. I'll just keep grinding, babe, and we'll see what happens. That in itself will show Carlito the diligent discipline and dedication he'll need to be whatever he wants to be. Also, we won't have to rely solely on the off-chance of me writing a block-buster hit to teach him that," he said, smiling. "This is really tasty, by the way. Thank you."

The next day, Daniel went through the same arduous morning commute. When he arrived at his office building, he greeted the security guards as affably as every other morning and then walked over to the elevator vestibule. He saw someone he hadn't ever seen in the building before, an older gentleman who looked noticeably disheveled. He didn't seem homeless exactly, just sloppy and unkempt. The dress shirt he had on under his colorful knit sweater was half tucked in, half out. One shoelace was untied. His hair was messy, and none of his clothing seemed to match. He was carrying two bulky bags that didn't seem as heavy as they were uncomfortable to carry. He got into the elevator, and Daniel followed. There was, oddly enough for this time of the morning, no one else in this vestibule. The gentleman dropped two pristine white pieces of paper folded in the exact same way behind him.

Daniel picked them up. "Excuse me, sir, you dropped these."

"Oh, thank you, young man," the older gentleman replied as he pressed his floor number on the elevator panel. "They're just notes with a saying. A reminder of something. Good thing it wasn't cash, huh?"

"Ha ha, very true," Daniel said.

"Which is more important, though?" the older gentleman asked before he answered his own question. "Cash? Or staying tethered to what's important? It depends where you're planning to go, I guess."

That resonated with Daniel, but he didn't respond. He was lost in thought. Thoughts of security and money versus writing his dreams into reality were swirling around in his mind. He snapped out of it when the older gentleman said, "Looks like it's stuck," apparently referring to the elevator.

Daniel looked up at the floor numbers and then at the older gentleman, confused, because the numbers were going up as expected. He shrugged it off and, in an uncharacteristic display of his usual introverted self, decided to engage the old man further. "Do you mind if I ask you a question, sir?"

"No, son, not at all."

"What do you do when you constantly find yourself in a rut between having to decide between chasing down your dream or just letting it go for good? How do you get unstuck when you're in that place?" Daniel asked.

"Let go and let God, as they say," the older gentleman replied. "Though I'm not particularly religious myself...the truth in that saying shines through, doesn't it?"

"I guess so, but on a practical level, all that means is sit back and do nothing," Daniel replied.

"Doing nothing is something," replied the older gentleman. "Having faith is also doing something. But pursuit without belief seems to be an exercise in futility to me. And it doesn't have to be a belief in some sort of divine intervention. It can be a belief in the process. Belief in yourself."

"What if I believe that after putting all of my eggs into one basket, I won't make it?" Daniel replied. "What if I chase down my dream of being a writer and I fail?"

"Let me ask you a question," replied the older gentleman. "How do you measure success? Is it fortune and fame? Riches beyond your wildest dreams, red carpet walks, and not being able to walk down the street without being noticed a half-dozen times by fans?"

"God no," Daniel replied. "I just want to do what I love and write when I want to write. I want to be able to provide for my family with my writing. Honestly, I prefer not to deal with any glitz and glamour."

"When was the last time you wrote?" the older gentleman asked.

"Last night," Daniel replied, "and, well, this morning a bit too, while on the subway ride here."

"And here, I presume, is where you work and generate the income to provide for your family, yes?" the older gentleman asked.

"Yes," Daniel replied.

"Then congratulations, son. You're already living your

dream. All you need is a perspective shift in order to realize it."

They arrived at Daniel's floor after what felt like a five-minute-long conversation and the doors opened. Daniel reached for his phone to check the time as he stepped out and, surprisingly noticed that no time had passed.

Daniel turned back and smiled. "Have a nice day, sir."

"Yes, yes," the older gentleman responded with a smile. "It is a good day to have a nice day."

"I see that now," replied Daniel. "Thank you."

"If you have any more questions," the older gentleman said right before the elevator doors closed, "I'm right above you."

Daniel put his phone back into his pocket and felt something. He pulled out a small but pristine white piece of paper and unfolded it to reveal a quote written there.

"Follow your dreams, they know the way." — Kobi Yamada

RATE & REVIEW

Did you enjoy this read?
Please don't forget to rate & review it at your favorite online
retailer!

About the Author

Tony Ortiz is a first-generation Dominican American born in Brooklyn and raised in Queens, New York. He is the host of the *Spun Today* Podcast, which is anchored in writing but unlimited in scope. He is a graduate of Baruch College in NYC and lives in Queens, New York with his wife and two sons.

facebook.com/SpunToday

twitter.com/SpunToday

instagram.com/SpunToday

youtube.com/@SpunToday

bookbub.com/authors/tony-ortiz

BOOKS BY THE AUTHOR

Make Way for You – Tips for Getting Out of Your Own Way

Fractal – A Time Travel Tale (A Novel)

Check out the following for even more reading:

Free-Writing: www.SpunToday.com/freewriting

Short Stories: www.SpunToday.com/shortstories

Sign up to my free weekly newsletter for a little boost to your day every Monday at noon. You can unsubscribe at any time, but you won't want to (I won't bombard you with spam, promise).

www.SpunToday.com/subscribe

SCAN ME

LISTEN TO MY PODCAST

Looking for a podcast that will take you on a thrilling ride of creativity and exploration? Look no further than the Spun Today Podcast, which is anchored in writing but unlimited in scope. Hosted by Tony Ortiz, this show is a celebration of the art of writing and so much more. With an endless range of interests and topics, Tony invites you to join him on a journey through the world of movies, books, TV shows, stand-up comedy, politics, MMA, current events, and beyond. Whether you're a fan of the written word or just looking for an exciting new podcast to add to your playlist, the Spun Today Podcast is the perfect choice. So why wait? Give it a whirl today and experience it for yourself!

Listen on Apple Podcasts, Spotify, YouTube, my website, or your favorite Pod-Catcher.

ACKNOWLEDGMENTS

To my father, Segundo Antonio Ortiz. You're the cornerstone of it all, Pop. You showed me that actions speak louder than words ever could. Thank you for teaching me the merits of integrity, discipline, responsibility, and hard work. These are invaluable character traits that I promise to pass on to the next generation. Making you proud means everything to me.

To my mother, Diomeda "Meme" Ortiz. Thank you for showing me humility and compassion. You've selflessly given all there is to give of you and truly made us a family. Your belief in me has always given me a reason to believe in myself.

To my big bro, David Ortiz. You've been hard on me when I didn't even know I needed you to be. For a long time, I felt like you were my biggest critic, until I realized you were by far my number one supporter. Thank you for always having my back and know that without hesitation I'll always have yours.

To my wife and babzy, Zoila Ortiz. If it wasn't for you, I probably wouldn't have ever taken this writing thing seriously. You made it all come together for me by giving me the nudge I needed to get on this journey, and you've been there every step of the way. Thank you for your unwavering kindness, unconditional love, and for showing me the importance of laughter. I had forgotten that some time ago.

You're my favorite person to be around and you constantly make me want to be a better me.

To my high school freshman English teacher, Ms. Lisa Gittlitz. You knew I should be writing before I ever did. I wish I would have listened more. Thank you for caring enough to always encourage this hard-headed teen and for making me write all those Lit-Logs.

To Maciel Gutierrez. If it weren't for you and a random conversation we had on an idle (I want to say Saturday) afternoon, I probably wouldn't have found the catharsis that comes with free-writing. Thank you for teaching me what it was and for always being a friend. I still have that first piece you got me to write.

The Joe Rogan Experience Podcast was the motivating straw that broke the procrastinating camel's back for me. It has been a hub of fascinating conversations, inspiration, fun times, and life lessons. Not only did it make me realize that it was okay to pursue my dreams, but it gave me the necessary kick in the ass to realize that they were all possible too. It's truly a gift that each of you should unwrap. Joe, Brian, Jaime, and every guest who has and continues to share their experiences on the show...thank you. I am eternally grateful.

I heard Elliott Hulse speak of the three types of people in our lives (you can find the video on YouTube). I reflected on the relationships in my life and found there to be a lot of truth to this. The concept really resonated with me. The gist of it is that the people in your life generally fall under one of these three categories:

Crystal balls: These are people through which you can see your future. Through them you ask yourself if you want to experience and characterize what this person represents, in your own future. Good, bad, or neutral.

Mirrors: These are people who give you back what you give them. You may see in them similar traits or goals and ambitions, which cause you to enjoy each other's company. Or you see people you're repelled by, and these can be people who themselves are reflecting back to you, traits in yourself that you need to address and rectify.

Angels: These are people who positively impact your life knowingly or not, and whether you're ready to receive their blessing(s) or not.

Each of you have touched my life in a significant way somewhere along the line, and fall under some combination of the above: Steven Almonte (the definition of a hustler), Frank "Steve" Padilla (thank you for being family), Jonathan Jacob (the only person I can reconnect with every couple years and have it feel as if we spoke the day before, without skipping a beat), Arnaldo Coutinho (a true mentor), Jose Luis Oliveira (who taught me: "don't leave for tomorrow what you can get done today"), Yudy Azurdia (la mejor decoradora de casa), Jacey Rosa (who has the best laugh), Raul Azurdia (the #1 Roomy), Omar "Jerry Rivera" Fuentes, Janet Velez (who deserves a trophy for holding down my brother), Jorge Nobre (thanks for going out of your way to drive me back from Mineola to Queens when we worked at the bar together), Benny Collado (blair-witz), Elaine Almonte (who I can always count on for an objective writing critique), Esrin Garcia (for teaching me how to really drive a stick-shift), Pablo Mosquera (for grabbing life by the handle bars), Peter Cepeda, Virginia Florentino, Raul Lizardo, Rafael Polanco, David "Energizer" Carvalho, Roberto Prudencio (¡ó

Algarve!), Arturo Flores (RIP), Dr. Arthur Lewin (my ambassador of Black & Latino studies), Jessica Florentino, Don Eladio (RIP), Doña Ana, Marisol & Antonio Almeida, Juana "Titi Mery" Susana, Maria "Titi Maro" Susana, Rafael "Mickey" Susana, Pedro "Julio" Susana, Ligia Reynoso, Francisco Reynoso (*da tuyo*), Reina "Tía Tata" Ortiz, Claribel & Julie Lizardo, Mary Reyes, Leonel Lucas, Abismael Gonzalez, Vicente Gonzalez *y todos mis Tíos, Tías, primos y familia.*

And last but certainly not least the future generation of the Ortiz Clan:

To my niece and goddaughter, Emma Ortiz. You have a heart of gold, and it shows. Don't let anyone or anything ever make you feel as if that's a bad thing. It's your greatest strength, and the future generation of our family is lucky to have you leading it.

To my niece, Olivia Ortiz. You're full of life and have a smile that brightens up any room. Keep smiling even when you're sad and know how infectious it is. You make others happier just by being around.

To both of my boys, which are pieces of my heart on the outside of my body:

To my big boy, Aiden Ortiz. You're an absolute blessing. My hope for you is that this book helps you realize there are alternative pathways you can take toward your version of happiness, and if you're willing to work 2, 3, 4 times as hard, you won't have to compromise responsibility to achieve it, either. Like your grandpa always said, "*Todo se puede hacer dentro de las reglas.*" Thank you for looking at me with the kindest eyes in the world. I love you.

To my baby boy, Grayson Ortiz. You know what you want and you're going to get it. Just make sure you channel that energy wisely and never lose the essence of you in the process of chasing down your dreams. Continue to be as thoughtful as you are. That's a strength of yours. Choose that charming smile of yours and go in the direction of your happiness. Thank you for letting me in. I love you.

*Substitute the mysticism with hard work
and start taking steps in the general direction of your dreams.*